BOSS'S PRETEND WIFE

A SECRET BABY ROMANCE

CRYSTAL MONROE

First rule of a fake marriage?
Don't get knocked up.

When my chiseled-by-God boss calls me to his office,
I think I'm about to get fired.
But instead, CEO Bryce Hollis proposes.
Marry him for six months,
Fix his playboy reputation so he won't lose his company,
And collect a giant bag of cash.

I'm game. How hard could it be?
Answer: very.
Because from the moment he kisses me at our fake wedding,
I know my V-card won't last long.
Neither will the wall I built around my heart.

When two pink lines show up on the pregnancy test stick,
I'm toast.
Because I want more than just pretend from Bryce.
I want him to love me for real.

Rule number two?
Never, ever, fall for your fake husband.

CHAPTER 1

CORA

"*B*ryce Hollis, you're all man."

I cringed. I hadn't meant to say that out loud, even if I'd only whispered it.

No one had heard me, thankfully. I was alone in the copy room. Still, I should have been able to look at a picture of my new boss without losing my shit.

But that was what Bryce Hollis did to women.

I worked for a total hottie. I'd never met him in person, but I knew every detail of his face.

And I wasn't a stalker, I swear. Gossip websites ran stories on him every few days. It wasn't hard to know what the man looked like.

Every perfect, bulging muscle.

My heart sped up as I stared at the picture of him on my phone. Another article about his latest playboy antics was making the rounds on social media.

Bryce Hollis, LA's most notorious bachelor, spent the weekend with three calendar models—Miss June, Miss July, and Miss August. This business mogul has a good time all year long.

I shook my head, minimized the article, and tucked my

phone back into my pocket while I waited for the copy machine to finish.

God, the man was an Adonis. He knew how to turn heads, and it wasn't just his perfect physique that did the trick.

When Bryce wasn't dating supermodels, he was throwing insane parties or pulling daredevil stunts with his friends. He gave celeb websites plenty to gossip about.

Ogling photos of the mysterious CEO at my new job was a fun distraction. Nothing more. Hollis Marketing was a big company, and I'd probably never even see the guy.

Get a grip, Cora, I scolded myself. *Drooling over photos of your boss is just weird.*

The copy machine finished with a thud. I took the stack of papers, adding them to my growing pile. Loading the tower of folders in my arms, I trudged out of the copy room.

I could barely see over the huge stack, but I didn't have time to carry them in smaller batches like a normal person.

I left normal a long time ago. Somewhere along the way, my nice, calm life turned crazy. I was just trying to keep up.

My supervisor Dana was waiting for the files. And in the month I'd been at this job, I'd learned that patience wasn't her strong suit. She always had a look on her face that said, "Make one more wrong move, and your ass is grass."

I might have been an intern and just one tiny step up from working in the mailing room, but damn it, that one step up *meant* something.

I was not going to lose this job.

My phone rang. I fished it out of my pocket and pinched it between my ear and shoulder while I hustled along the corridor.

"Did you die?" Dana snapped over the phone.

"No, I'm on my way."

"I need those files yesterday."

"I know," I said. "I'll be right there. I just had to—"

She hung up before I could finish my sentence. I rolled my eyes, dropped the phone on top of the stack of files, and hurried on.

I answered to Dana directly. To say that we didn't get along was an understatement. She was a pain in my ass. But I was just an intern. I was lucky I got paid at all.

Suck it up for a while longer, I told myself like a mantra.

This was temporary, just until someone at Hollis Marketing noticed that I was capable of more than file hustling and fetching coffee. Then I would be golden.

I tried not to dwell on the fact that I'd spent four long years in college to get a job that was better than this. If I hadn't taken a two-year break after college to take care of my mom, my life would have been different.

But I couldn't get lost in *what ifs.*

I was going to keep this ship afloat, no matter what it took. Even if some days felt more impossible than others.

I rounded the corner and picked up the pace, mentally rehearsing my apology to Dana.

Then, *bam.*

I ran smack into someone. Someone *big.*

I yelped, falling backward. The files flew across the floor with a crash.

Great.

"What the hell?" I snapped in irritation. I looked up the expensive suit pants and the broad chest to the perfect face looking down at me.

The face that had been on the covers of magazines and tabloids for months. The one I'd been drooling over on my phone just a moment ago.

The face of the man who owned Hollis Marketing.

Bryce Hollis, who I thought I'd never see in person, was standing above me. And I was sprawled on the floor like a lunatic.

"Oh, shoot," I said, shaking my head. "I mean, I'm sorry. I didn't realize it was you. My mistake."

He chuckled and held out a hand to help me to my feet. I tried—and failed—to look ladylike as I struggled in my narrow pencil skirt. When I stood, I scraped the blonde hair out of my face and straightened my clothes.

It was safe to say he was larger than life in person.

And handsome. *God.* Drop. Dead. Gorgeous.

Dark blond hair, blue eyes that pierced my soul, and when he cocked a smile at me, I felt woozy. He was about to make me lose my balance for the second time.

"Weren't you ever taught not to run in hallways?" he asked, the corners of his mouth pulling up.

He sounded amused, not angry. Thank goodness. I was pretty sure I could get fired for snapping at the boss like that. And for running into him.

Not that I could have done any damage to Bryce. The man was built like a freight train—muscles in all the right places. Solid, taut, *delicious.*

What was wrong with me? I couldn't lust after the man who owned the company. Not while he was standing right in front of me.

"I, uh… no. I mean, yeah. I know I shouldn't run in the hall. But Ms. Blevins needs these files, like, yesterday." I cringed. *I sound like an idiot.* "And she's scary." *And like a child.*

Mr. Hollis chuckled. "Well, let's not keep her waiting then, shall we?"

He kneeled to gather my files together. I kneeled, too, grabbing the files as he handed them to me. His fingers brushed against mine, and electricity danced over my skin.

Get a grip, Cora.

"Thank you, Mr. Hollis," I said, straightening. He stood, too, and towered over me once more. How tall was he? He had to be well over six feet.

"Call me Bryce."

I blushed. Like a *teenager.* "Bryce."

He chuckled again. "And you are?"

"Oh, Cora. Rhodes. I'm… the new intern."

Why the hell did I say that?

He grinned at me. "Yeah, I can tell you're new."

"How?"

He shrugged. "You have that jumpy attitude the new employees have, like you're trying a little too hard."

Wonderful. He thinks I'm clueless. "I'm just… trying to make a good impression."

He reached for me, and I stiffened. He brushed a strand of hair out of my face.

Oh my God. Bryce Hollis just touched my *hair.*

"Well, it's working," he said in that deep voice.

I blushed harder. My cheeks were probably scarlet by now. Judging from the amusement in his eyes, I was pretty sure I was right.

"Well, Cora," he said. "It was nice running into you."

"Technically, I ran into you," I pointed out in a breathy voice.

When he raised his eyebrows slightly, I blushed again. I was being a fool. Not only was this man so hot I couldn't think straight, he was also the owner of the company, and a man who was known to make women swoon.

"I have to go," I said and hurried past him. I was fully aware that I was probably being rude, but I was at a complete loss for what to say.

Did I just have a moment with Bryce Hollis?

I wanted desperately to glance over my shoulder to see if he was watching me walk away. But I couldn't do it. No way in hell could I risk the embarrassment.

I pushed Dana's door open with my shoulder and carefully put the files down in front of her.

She looked at me with an unimpressed expression. "Did you stop for a cup of coffee on the way?"

I shook my head. "I dropped the files. They… may have gotten out of order. I'm so sorry."

"You're kidding."

"I can re-order them back at my desk?" I offered, wincing.

"You've done enough," Dana said with a glare. "Just go."

She shooed me out of her office with a flick of her wrist. I slunk back to my cubicle in the large office space down the hall from where Dana was stationed. With a groan, I collapsed into my chair.

"She's not going to be a bitch to you forever, you know," Avery said on the other side of the partition. She popped her head over to look at me, red hair falling over her shoulder.

"Somehow, I doubt that," I said. "I don't get the impression that she's going to take me any more seriously if I get a full-time position here."

"She's not so bad once you get to know her."

I wasn't so sure I wanted to know Dana Blevins any better than I knew her now. But I had bigger news to tell Avery.

She and I had been best friends since college. Avery had gotten me the interview for this intern position when I'd come up empty handed in my job search. I told her everything.

"You'll never guess who I just ran into," I whispered.

"Who?"

"Bryce Hollis."

Avery blinked at me. "Are you kidding me? Where? He's never down here. I mean, he's practically a king, always up on the top floor. He doesn't mix with us commoners." She looked around, trying to spot him on the floor.

I shrugged, trying to look nonchalant. Inside, I was reeling. "I'm serious. I *ran* into him. Like, physically. I dropped my files and he helped me pick them up."

"Oh, my God," Avery said, pressing her hand against her mouth for a moment. "It's like a movie."

"Yeah," I said with a sigh. "Except in movies, the woman doesn't act like a total spaz."

Avery laughed. "What did you say to him?"

"That I'm an intern." I closed my eyes and groaned.

"That's… um," Avery said, struggling for words. "Well, it's not good. But, I mean, now he knows where to find you."

"As if he would ever *try* to find me," I said and rolled my eyes.

Avery shook her head, her eyes bright with curiosity. "What did he say to you?"

"That I'm making a good impression."

"Really? That's *good.*"

I scoffed. "There's nothing good about that. Avery, he probably thought I was a total idiot. I mean, the guy dates supermodels and has red carpet shoots with celebrities. I'm nobody. He probably forgot who I was before I scurried past him."

Avery shook her head, her face unbelieving. "I think it's pretty cool. It's like going to the store and accidentally bumping into someone famous, you know?"

"I *did* bump into someone famous," I pointed out.

Bryce Hollis had to be the most famous—or *infamous*—bachelor that LA's business world had ever seen. And he'd only been CEO for six months, since his dad retired and left the company to him.

Avery giggled. "Exactly."

Dana walked out of her office, passing by our cubicle. Avery ducked back behind her partition. We both pretended to work until Dana was out of sight.

When she was gone, Avery popped over the partition again, pulled a goofy face at me, and ducked back down.

I laughed and shook my head before getting down to work.

Call me Bryce.

It was better to forget about Bryce Hollis. I would probably never see him again. Even if I did, he wasn't the type of guy that would notice someone like me. I was nobody. The bottom of the food chain at this company.

And he was like a Greek god, chiseled by angels and sent to Earth for glamorous, beautiful women. Women who were nothing like me.

Besides, it wasn't like men were an option for me, anyway. I wasn't interested in relationships. I had to focus on my work.

I earned next to nothing as an intern. If I didn't land a permanent job soon, my mom and I were going under. Everything was resting on my shoulders now that I was the only one able to work. Since she'd gotten sick, it was up to me to pay all the bills. And our measly medical insurance didn't cover everything.

If I finally got a good job, I could cover all the bills at once, instead of guessing which company wouldn't breathe down my neck right away.

Dating wasn't in the cards for me. At least not now. Men had never done me or my mom any good anyway. Not my dad, who'd left my mom when she was pregnant with me, and not the few jerks I'd attempted to date in college.

My attention was laser focused on one thing: earning enough money to keep our heads above water.

Bryce Hollis, with his string of supermodel girlfriends, was the last thing I needed to think about.

The rest of the day passed in a blur. Dana kept me busy running around for her. Avery, who was a permanent employee and above coffee runs, left at three to visit a client. As the afternoon dragged on, the office emptied out. Soon, I was the only one left on the floor. I didn't get overtime as an intern, but I often worked late to prove I was serious about this job.

My head buzzed after the long day. With a sigh, I grabbed my phone and opened my grocery list. My mom had remote access to the list, and she added items we needed. I hoped there wouldn't be anything urgent to buy today.

No such luck.

Toilet paper!! had been added to the top of the list. The exclamation marks meant we were almost out.

Shit.

With a deep breath, I opened my banking app. I had a nagging feeling my account was almost empty.

My stomach clenched as I saw the balance. The little left over from the babysitting gigs I'd taken in the last two years was earmarked to keep our lights on. I couldn't make a supply run until my first payday next week.

To feed us, I could make do with what we had in the fridge. I'd gotten us by with cabbage soup and stale bread more than once.

But toilet paper? That wasn't something I could fabricate out of thin air. And we sure as hell couldn't stretch it any more than we already did.

What was I going to do? I scrubbed my face with my hands. And suddenly got an idea.

Everyone had left already, right? And the cleaning crew put new toilet paper rolls into the stalls every morning before the staff came in. If I were to take one or two, no one would notice. They would just replace them in the morning.

I squeezed my eyes shut. I *hated* this. But I had to take care of Mom and me. And I had to bring essential items like toilet paper home. Otherwise, Mom would know the truth about our finances.

I hadn't been completely honest with her about how fast we'd gone through our savings. She had more than enough to worry about already. Stress didn't help her cancer recovery.

Protecting my mom from the truth was another burden on my shoulders.

I rose from my desk and packed my things before walking to the bathroom. My heart pounded as I made sure the stalls were all empty. A stack of rolls, all wrapped in packaging, perched on the counter. Before I could change my mind, I took two and stuffed them into my purse. The second roll was visible from the top, I realized with apprehension.

But with my coat causally thrown over the bag, no one would notice. I just had to exit the building and head straight to my car.

When I walked out of the restroom, I felt sick to my stomach. I wasn't a thief. I wasn't someone who believed I was entitled to something I didn't work my fingers to the bone for.

I'll replace the toilet paper, I promised myself. Even if no one noticed it was gone in the first place.

I'm just borrowing it.

The elevator doors pinged and slid open on the ground floor. I walked into the lobby.

"Cora," a familiar voice said.

My eyes landed right on Bryce Hollis. Again.

And just like that, he was by my side. So close I could smell his cologne.

"Hi," I said, swallowing hard.

"Twice in one day, huh?" he said. "Working late?"

I nodded, painfully aware of the rolls of paper hiding under my coat.

"Admirable. You're doing great keeping up that good impression." He winked at me, his mouth pulling into a knowing smile. My insides melted a little.

I cleared my throat. "Thanks. Have a good evening, Mr. Hollis."

"Bryce," he reminded me. "And let me walk you to your car."

"You don't have to do that," I said.

Bryce was gorgeous, but I just wanted to get away. He made me feel like a fluttery schoolgirl.

"I insist," he said.

His green eyes locked on mine as he towered above me like a god. I opened my mouth to refuse, but I couldn't speak.

Say no, Cora. My lips moved without words, like a fish.

Damn it.

"Okay."

We turned toward the door. When Bryce opened it for me, a cold gust of wind sliced through my clothes. I gasped. My arms broke out in goosebumps, and I shivered.

"It's not summer just yet," Bryce said, whistling through his teeth. When he looked at me, he frowned. "You're freezing."

"I'm fine," I said, but my teeth started chattering. God, I was a terrible liar.

Bryce grinned. "Here," he said, and he grabbed my coat. In the process, my handbag slipped from my shoulder. I watched in horror as the top toilet paper roll fell out and rolled away.

Of course.

I cringed.

Bryce looked down, frowning. He bent to pick it up. "What's this?" he asked.

My throat felt like it was going to close. "I... uh... it's toilet paper."

He raised his eyebrows. "I can see that. Why is it in your bag?"

I bit my lip. "I have no idea how that got there!" My cringe deepened. Yeah, that wasn't going to work. And judging by the way he was looking at me, he didn't buy it, either.

I let out a breath. "I took it from the restroom."

"You're stealing from me?"

God, he was making it sound so personal. I wasn't exactly stealing from *him*. But since it was his company, I guess I was, indirectly.

"I'm sorry," I said. "I was going to replace it later. I just don't have the money for supplies and groceries right now. If I don't go home with it, my mom will know how low our bank account is and that we're in a mess. I just need to keep up this front a little longer until I get my paycheck." I felt like an idiot for blabbing to him. But at least I was telling him the truth.

"You don't have money for groceries?" Bryce asked, looking confused.

I swallowed hard and shook my head.

"No, I don't." A mix of shame and humiliation swept through me. "Are you going to fire me?"

Bryce looked shocked. "Are you kidding me?"

"I won't blame you if you do. It's wrong to steal, even if I was going to replace it. I just can't go home empty-handed, please—"

"Cora," Bryce said and grinned. "It's fine. It's just toilet paper. Seriously. And this…" He looked at the roll he was still holding. "This is the cheap stuff. Here." He handed it to me and took his wallet from his back pocket. I watched in a daze as he pulled out a handful of bills and pressed them into my hand. "Buy yourself the good stuff, okay?"

"I… I…" I hesitated, staring at the money. I didn't count it right then, but there were multiple hundred-dollar bills. I could tell it was a small fortune. "I can't take this." I held it back out to him.

"Don't be ridiculous. Take it, get what you need."

I frowned. "Why are you being so nice?"

Bryce's face darkened a little. "Just because people think I'm an ass for not living up to their expectations, doesn't mean I can't be nice sometimes."

"Oh, I didn't mean it that way—"

"It's fine. That's not on you. But take it, and do what you need to do, Cora. Don't worry about paying it back, either."

I swallowed hard, a lump suddenly rising in my throat.

Bryce's phone rang, and he looked irritated when he looked at the caller ID. "I have to go. I'll see you around, Cora."

He turned on his heel and left me standing in the parking lot, trying to figure out what had just happened.

"Bye, Bryce," I whispered as I came to my senses. I counted the money and gasped.

Bryce Hollis had given me five hundred dollars.

Bewildered, I tucked the money into my wallet then walked to my rundown Toyota sedan. I was glad he hadn't seen my twenty-year-old clunker.

I turned the key in the ignition. Today was definitely my lucky day—even my car started on the first try.

Relief flooded through me as I thought about the money Bryce had given me. His devilish grin flashed in my mind, sending butterflies through my belly.

I had a feeling tonight wouldn't be the last time I saw Bryce Hollis.

And I wasn't sure whether I should be thrilled or terrified about running into him again.

CHAPTER 2

*D*ad's timing was literally the worst.

I stormed back inside the building, irritated by his little surprise. Dad had entered my office while I was away and then called and demanded a meeting.

Right when I was talking to the cute intern.

But Sal Hollis wasn't a man who liked to be kept waiting. I could blow off a lot of people, but there was no putting off my father. It didn't matter that I was now CEO.

While I rode the elevator, I thought about Clumsy Cora and grinned. God, she was something else. As if the little incident with the files hadn't been amusing enough this morning, her toilet paper theft was a new level of entertaining. It had been a long time since I'd met a woman who drew my attention like that.

It wasn't just because she was clumsy, either. She was nothing like any of the women I'd been with. She was just… different.

And incredibly beautiful. Long blonde hair, a pixie face and those big, doe eyes. Innocent. Though her sweet, round ass made me want to do *filthy* things to her.

And the way she kept blushing. When was the last time a woman had blushed when I complimented her? It must have been years. The women I spent time with believed they were God's gift to mankind.

Cora was nothing like that. Shy, sweet, modest. And that made me want her. *Badly.*

But that wasn't going to happen. Not with this one. She was way too innocent, despite her petty office crime. She would likely notify HR if I so much as flirted with her.

It was a shame.

The elevator doors opened on the top floor.

"He's in your office, sir," Terri, my secretary, said. She was a workhorse and always the last employee to leave at night.

"What mood is he in?" I asked.

Terri offered me wide eyes.

I was in deep shit. But I should have known. This was the first time Dad had come to the office since I'd taken over as CEO six months ago. Something was wrong.

My dad had prepped me to take over his company my entire life. Now, at thirty, I was finally in charge.

Or, at least, I was the new figurehead. My dad was still the Big Guy behind the scenes, telling me how to run his empire, how to sail his fucking ship.

I had a feeling I knew what this meeting was about. He'd come here to shit all over me about my most recent scandal: the publicity about the models. Miss June, Miss July, *and* Miss August. It had been one endless summer, all in one weekend.

A man didn't turn down a dare, and there wasn't a woman out there I couldn't get. Five thousand bucks had proven me right. My buddy Chaz was probably still pissed off about it.

Man, it had been a hell of a weekend. But truth be told, I'd gotten bored after June. They were all the same. And I didn't mean because they'd been chosen as calendar models, either.

Hookups were getting to be tedious.

I was shocked at the thought. But it was true.

Women slept with me because I was Bryce Hollis, the man about town with more money than he knew what to do with. I was a notch in their bedposts as much as they were one in mine. I didn't remember their names any longer than I needed to—when I forgot, a substitute like baby, honey, or sweetheart worked just fine. And they weren't interested in getting to know me, either. Not the real me.

Lately, I was just going through the motions.

When I got to my office, I froze in the doorway. My dad was seated behind the desk. *My* desk.

That pissed me off. But it had been *his* desk just a few months ago, so I shrugged it off. I sat down opposite him, like a guest in my own office.

"To what do I owe the pleasure?" I asked.

"You know why I'm here."

I sighed. "It's because of the women, isn't it?" It was *always* about the women.

"I don't know why it gives you so much pleasure to piss me off, Bryce. But it's not about me. It's about the company."

I snorted and rolled my eyes. "What I do with my personal life—and who I sleep with—has nothing to do with the company."

"No, you're right," my dad said, steepling his fingers. "It's the fact that you have to get it on the news every damn time. *That's* the problem. You can't just screw around behind closed doors, can you? You have to let the world know that you have a dick and you know how to use it."

I chuckled at my dad's use of language. He didn't swear unless he was completely pissed.

"Is something funny?" he asked.

16

I shrugged. "I just don't see what this has to do with the company."

"The board of directors are pissed, Bryce. They see the news, too. And they're not happy."

"Because they can't get laid themselves?"

My dad slammed his fist on my desk, making my stationery jump. "This isn't a fucking joke! I know you don't give a shit about this company. Maybe you're happy to piss it away the first chance you get, but I put my blood, sweat, and tears into this place to leave you a legacy."

I clenched my jaw, my anger rising my match my dad's. I was a lot of things—a disappointment, a son of a bitch, a womanizer. But I *did* care about the company.

My dad took a deep breath, trying to get himself under control.

"Asking you to change won't work. God knows I've talked to you about this a thousand times. So, I'm bringing in a publicist to get this company's image back on track."

"You *what?*" I asked, the anger replaced by shock.

"You heard me." My dad looked up at the door. As if on cue, a woman walked in. She was older but in decent shape. Her dark hair was pulled back into a tight ponytail, and she had sharp eyes.

"This is Allison Evans," my dad said. "This type of thing is her specialty."

Ms. Evans nodded at me. "It's a pleasure, Bryce. We'll be working together as I help manage your public relations."

"I don't think that's necessary," I said.

"And I don't give a shit," my dad snapped. "Allison is here to keep you on the straight and narrow so that you don't sink a company I worked thirty years to build. The investors are threatening to pull out, Bryce. Two of them have hinted about looking for greener pastures. That makes the board of directors nervous. Son, it's *your* job to keep investors interested and the board members satisfied. It's time to start wooing them instead of these women you're so fond of."

I bristled. I wasn't my dad—he did business differently than I ever would. But just because I didn't do things the way he would, and because I fucked around, didn't mean that I didn't work hard. The company was just as important to me as it was to my father.

"What am I supposed to do?" I asked with a sigh. If he needed me to work with this woman to prove that I was serious about the company, I would do it. Whatever. How damn hard could it be?

"Do you know what's in your contract, Bryce?" Allison asked.

I didn't like the way she talked to me. She spoke to me like I was a schoolboy who didn't understand how the world worked.

"Of course, I know what's in it," I said, trying not to sound as irritated as I felt.

"Then you're familiar with the morality clause."

I frowned. "Morality clause? That's for married employees. That's got nothing to do with me."

Allison glanced at my dad, who turned his head toward the window. He was washing his hands of the whole thing.

"The morality clause grants an employer the right to terminate the employment agreement based on an employee's conduct that adversely impacts the company," she said without taking a breath.

I blinked at her. "Jesus, did you swallow a dictionary?" I grinned at my own joke, but Allison didn't seem impressed.

"Do you understand what that means?" she asked.

I sighed, the smile still on my face. "Yes, but I don't see how it applies to me."

"It means," my dad said, chipping in, "you're legally required to present a certain image."

I narrowed my eyes. "You want me to stop fucking around."

"Yeah," my dad said. "That's exactly it. If you don't do something about your playboy act, you're out of the company for good."

"I'm the CEO," I said defiantly. "Not an employee. Who's going to fire *me*?"

"I am," my dad said simply. "I may have retired and handed the company over to you. But if you don't get your shit together and start acting like the owner of Hollis Marketing, I'll get the board to vote you out, Bryce."

I was pissed off again. "You can't do that," I said.

But I knew my dad was right—he *could* do that. And he would. If there was anything that mattered to him in this world, it was his company. He could get rid of me—his only child—in the blink of an eye. But he would bend over backward to save his real baby: his business.

It had been that way since I was a kid.

"Did you forget the matter of the probation?" Dad asked.

My ears pricked up.

"Your father informed me of your year-long probation period," Allison offered. "During this time, the board of directors can have you removed if they feel it is necessary."

"Oh, yeah," I muttered. That did ring a bell. I'd somehow forgotten about it.

"Right," Dad said. "And you still have six months left of probation. So you better shape up quickly. And you better make it damned good, because Stark is hell-bent on getting you out of here."

"Fine," I said, standing and turning toward the door.

"Leaving so soon?" my dad asked.

"I don't see what more we have to discuss. You've made yourself clear. I've got to fix my playboy image." I glared at Allison. "Would getting married suffice?"

She blinked, surprised. So, it wasn't that hard to break that stony expression of hers.

"I… I guess it would. Yeah."

Dad snorted. "He's not serious. He's fucking with you."

"Send me a list of whatever it is I need to stop doing," I said. "Better yet, send me a list of what I *should* be doing, since that list would be shorter. Then I'll get started."

I turned around and left the office before either my dad or Allison Evans could respond.

"Goodnight, sir," Terri said from the desk when I walked to the elevator. I punched the button and stepped in without answering her, scowling as the doors slid shut.

I couldn't fucking believe it. A morality clause? I didn't remember that being in my contract. Then again, I'd never really read the damn thing. When my dad retired, I'd signed on the dotted line to get what was coming to me, and that was that. I hadn't thought I would have to pore over it with my lawyer. It was a family business, for God's sake.

But then, my dad had been the one to draw up the contract in the first place. Maybe that should have been warning enough that I'd needed to check it out.

I bristled as I rode my way down to the lobby. Fucking playboy image. I wouldn't be allowed to have any fun if I wanted to please the board and the investors. And there was no way in hell I was walking away. I *did* care about this company. I may have acted like a party kid sometimes, but I was also a damned hard worker. My business meant the world to me.

If I lost it, there'd be nothing left for me. *I* would be lost.

That settled it, then. I'd just have to conform to this fucked-up image they wanted from me. I could do anything for six months.

But simply staying out of nightclubs wouldn't be enough for the board of directors. I'd already known they were looking for any excuse to force me out. I just hadn't known how easy it would be for them with the morality clause. After the shenanigans with the three models, they may have been already working behind the scenes to vote me out.

I had to act fast. And I had to make it spectacular.

The elevator doors pinged, and I crossed the lobby. When I stepped out of the building, the wind drove through my coat and I flipped my collar up. Clumsy Cora popped into my mind. Despite the hellish meeting I'd just had, I couldn't help but smile.

The smile faded again when I thought about my public image and how I would have to stop dicking around.

Cora was the type of woman even Allison Evans would approve of.

As I climbed into my car, a light bulb went off in my head.

Maybe getting married wasn't such a bad idea.

I'd been sarcastic when I asked the publicist about marriage. But now, a wife was looking better and better. Someone who could keep up the act for a while, make me look like the good guy. It wouldn't be forever, right? People got divorced all the time.

If I could get someone wholesome and sweet to pose as my wife, and get the board members off my back, then I could pull it off.

And Clumsy Cora was the perfect woman for the job.

CHAPTER 3

*B*ryce kept sneaking into my thoughts. And not just because he was hot as hell.

I'd made a total fool of myself, and he'd been more than gallant. The man had caught me in the act of petty theft. Of all things! But he'd been nothing but a knight in shining armor about it. That made me melt all over again when I replayed the scene in my mind as I drove home.

I parked in front of the modest house I shared with my mom and took a deep breath, letting it out slowly. I was a mess of emotions—embarrassed he'd caught me but relieved I could have electricity *and* food this month.

I didn't want my mom to see me like this. I had to be strong so she could focus on getting better.

When she'd been diagnosed with advanced breast cancer two years ago, my world had crashed down.

She meant everything to me. My dad had ditched her before I was born. He'd been a non-entity in my life. I didn't even know what the guy looked like. Forget about getting a card or a call on my birthday—much less seeing him every other weekend like other kids did with their fathers.

Alimony or child support to help me or my mom out all those years? Ha!

It was just me and Mom against the world.

For years, she'd worked three jobs to keep us going. Shortly after her diagnosis, I dropped all my plans to do the same for her.

I had just graduated college with great job prospects in advertising. But Mom's surgery and other treatments had made her weak as a kitten. There was no one else to help out, no other family or friends that could give her the full-time care she needed. So I'd been the one to step up. I'd turned down job offers to take care of her. And I never thought twice about it.

By some miracle, she was finally in remission now. But she was still too weak to work. She got better every day, but she had a long road ahead.

And until she could walk out of here on her two feet and work full days again, I'd scramble as much as I needed to. It was time for me to repay her for everything she'd done for me.

She deserved it more than anyone I knew.

And she didn't need to witness my emotional roller coaster on top of it all. I didn't want to burden her.

Which was why I hadn't told her how bad our finances had become. I'd taken on odd jobs the past two years whenever I could—pet sitting and babysitting. It helped a little. But without a steady income for two years, we'd blown through the little savings we had and maxed out our credit cards.

I didn't tell her that we were in a hole. I was going to get us out of it, so the worry would be unnecessary, and the stress would only hinder her recovery.

Unfortunately, those great job offers had dried up. After being out of school and the workforce for two years, the internship at Hollis Marketing was the best I could find. The silver lining was that the company paid its full-time employees well. If I could only last long enough to get hired permanently, I'd be able to keep us afloat.

My only worry was we'd run out of money before then.

When the front door opened—she'd probably heard my car—I plastered a smile on my face and hopped out.

"I have a surprise," I said and opened the trunk.

My mom slowly came to the car. I watched her carefully, looking for telltale signs that she was sick, that something was wrong or hurting. But she didn't look like she was in a lot of pain right now, and despite her shuffling walk and her painfully slow movements, there was color in her cheeks.

She peered into the trunk, taking in the glorious sight of several shopping bags loaded with food and household supplies. I hadn't been able to afford such a big grocery run in ages, and the trunk full of food was a relief to us both. Her eyes widened, and she lifted her hands to her cheeks.

"Where did you get all of this?" she asked.

"At the grocery store, Mom," I said, rolling my eyes in mock sarcasm. But I was grinning. I kissed her on the cheek. "Why don't you go inside while I bring this in? I'll make us supper."

"Oh, sweetheart," Mom said. Her eyes were watery. "I thought we were struggling more than you were letting on, but this…" Her voice trailed off. I patted her on the shoulder.

"I told you, I've got this."

A pang of guilt shot through me for lying to her. But at the moment, it didn't matter. I had to keep Mom out of the loop for her own good.

She shuffled her way inside again while I carried the groceries to the kitchen and filled the pantry and fridge. The shelves had been empty for a long time, and a full refriger-

ator brought joy to my heart. I'd bought healthy food, too—
fruits and vegetables and meat.

After I unpacked it all, she insisted on helping me cook.
Mom tired easily, but she sat at the breakfast nook and
chopped salad ingredients while I stewed chicken and
roasted root vegetables. The smell in the kitchen made my
stomach rumble.

We enjoyed the first decent meal we'd shared in weeks,
and she laughed as I told her the highlights of my day. I did
not mention my two run-ins with Bryce Hollis.

After we ate, Mom looked like she'd used all her energy.
She started fading on the couch. I shook her gently and she
blinked her eyes open.

"Let's get you to bed, Mom," I said.

"Oh, but it's so early," she said, stifling a yawn. "It thought
we could watch a movie together. I see so little of you these
days."

"We'll watch one tomorrow," I said when she yawned
again.

She nodded. "Maybe you're right. I'm still a little under
the weather."

A little was an understatement. Rachel Rhodes was a shell
of the woman she'd once been. Before, she'd been vibrant
and strong. Now, she was skin and bones, and she wore out
so easily. But she was getting better. She'd started eating
more and sleeping well, and I had high hopes that she would
stay on top of this thing. She'd beaten cancer. I just needed
her to keep fighting.

After making sure my mom had taken her meds and was
tucked into bed, I walked back to the living room and started
clearing up. When I put away a few loose items that had been
lying around, I happened on a stack of envelopes I'd received
a while ago and forgotten about.

Some of them had angry red stamps on them. I swallowed hard, my stomach turning as I sat down on the couch.

I opened the envelopes one by one. As I read the words, my stomach sank and I felt sick.

I could pay the gas and water bills with the remainder of the money Bryce had given me, and I could manage the minimum payments on the medical bills and the insurance on my car, but the mortgage...

My hand gripped my stomach as it churned in anxiety.

I hadn't realized how far I'd fallen behind. I had a past-due notice on the mortgage, and they were far less forgiving than some of the other services I took a chance on from time to time.

I pressed my hand against my forehead.

It's going to be okay, I tried to convince myself.

Until I opened the last letter.

A letter of foreclosure on the house. Proceedings would begin next week.

The blood drained from my face. The world around me tilted a little before righting itself. I'd known I was late paying the mortgage, but I hadn't realized it was this serious.

We couldn't lose the house—where the hell would we go? We had no other family to turn to. My mom had been an only child, like me, and her parents had passed away years ago. I had no contact with my dad's side of the family. Hell, I wouldn't even know where to start looking if leaning on them was an option at all.

I covered my face with my hands and tried to bite back tears. I needed a miracle. If we lost the house, everything I'd been fighting for would crumble. I couldn't let my mom down. I'd been working my ass off. Failure was not an option.

Something had to give.

Instead of allowing myself to fall apart, I got up and did

what I *could* do. I paid the gas bill, the minimum amount on the medical bills, and the car insurance. I sat at the table with a calculator, trying to figure out how I could swing the mortgage.

I just didn't make enough money. Maybe I could take on more babysitting jobs. I could work three jobs at once. Or should I focus my efforts on applying for a new marketing job and hope it would pay more?

But there was no good solution. Every employer wanted someone with experience, which I didn't have much of. And even if I worked around the clock doing odd jobs, I still couldn't pay off the mounting bills.

Defeated, I crawled into bed. I squeezed my eyes shut, praying that it would all go away.

My mom was still sleeping when I left the house the next morning. I was relieved I didn't have to put on a brave face in front of her when I felt like crying. I was sick with worry. If I fell apart in front of my mom, she would know something was seriously wrong. I couldn't do that to her.

It was easier to pretend at the office where almost no one knew me well. Even Avery, who knew most of what I was going through, was unaware of just how bad things had become.

When I arrived at my desk, Avery was already there. She looked excited.

"So, Bryce Hollis was here, looking for you," she said right away.

"What?" My stomach turned again. Had he changed his mind about the theft? About the money? Surely he didn't want me to pay him back. "What did he want?"

"Why the hell would he tell me that?" Avery asked. "He just said you should go to his office when you get in."

"Oh," I said. I wiped my sweaty palms on my skirt.

"What do you think it's about?" Avery asked excitedly. She

27

couldn't see how this could be a bad thing. Oh, if only she knew.

"I don't know," I lied. Because I was pretty sure I knew what this was about. I was sure he'd had a change of heart.

"Go!" Avery said. "Don't keep the man waiting. It's Bryce Hollis, for God's sake!"

I nodded, swallowed hard, and tried to offer Avery a smile that failed miserably before I walked to the elevator and rode it to the top floor.

When the doors opened, I looked around. The top floor was nothing like the rest of the building—not that I'd been much higher up than my floor. The carpet beneath my feet was plush, my heels sinking into it when I walked to the reception desk. The waiting area had large leather couches, a fern that looked happier than any houseplant I'd ever seen, and a coffee station complete with a barista.

"Can I help you?" the receptionist asked with a polite smile. She had immaculate blonde hair, and her lips were a deep red. Even the employees on the top floor were fancy.

"I'm Cora Rhodes," I said. "I believe Mr. Hollis asked for me."

"You can go through, Miss Rhodes," she said with a smile that seemed genuine and warm. "He's waiting for you."

When she said that, my throat closed up and a wave of nausea rolled through me. As I walked to his office, passing what looked like a living room with a bar, and a conference room with armchairs and a large screen, I tried to rehearse what I would tell him.

I would pay back the money as soon as I was able. I would replace the toilet paper. I'd beg him not to fire me because my mom was sick. I just needed more time.

When I walked into Bryce's office, my steps faltered. It was even more luxurious than the rest of the floor, with full-length windows looking out over LA—there was even a glimpse of the ocean in the distance—and large bookcases filled with serious-looking books and leather-bound journals.

Bryce leaned against a large mahogany desk, arms folded over his chest as he looked out over the city. His sleeves were rolled up and his bicep muscles bulged. I forced myself not to stare and cleared my throat.

When he saw me, he pushed away from the desk and smiled.

"Cora," he said. His voice caressed my skin, and I tried to gauge his mood. He didn't look upset. That was a good start, right? "You can close the door."

I turned and did as he asked.

"Is it serious?" I blurted out when he didn't say anything.

He chuckled. "What?"

"I've never been called in here before. Am I in trouble? Is it about yesterday? I promise I—"

"It's not about yesterday, Cora," he interrupted me. "I need to talk to you."

"Okay," I said.

"Have a seat," he said, gesturing to one of two leather armchairs that faced his desk.

I sat down, perched on the edge of the expensive seat. He leaned against his desk again, holding the edge. My eyes grazed over his hands. They were *huge*. I quickly averted my eyes, determined to look *only* at his face. But I couldn't help but notice his broad shoulders and chiseled physique. That button-down shirt did little to hide his strong, commanding body.

I cleared my throat. A line of sweat appeared on my hairline as I shifted in my seat.

Great. Now I'm sweating in front of Bryce Hollis.

He studied my face for a long time, and I fought a blush. Was he just toying with me, watching me squirm?

I couldn't take it anymore. "Why am I here?" I finally asked.

"I helped you yesterday," he said.

I nodded slowly. "And I'm utterly grateful for it." God, was he going to hold that against me? I should have known. I hadn't thought that there would be strings attached. But with a man like Bryce—a man who probably had more women under his belt, literally, than there were employees in his firm—of course he would want something from me.

"Well, I need you to repay the favor," he said.

I was scared to ask, but I had to know.

"What is it?"

Sex? Probably sex. Oh, God. And I was a *virgin.* How the hell was I going to get out of this?

"Marry me," he said.

CHAPTER 4

"*E*xcuse me?"

Her jaw dropped, and I fought back a smile. My amusement at her wasn't appropriate at the moment. But something about those pink, full lips, parted in shock and confusion...

Well, it woke my cock up, that was for sure.

I walked around my desk to hide the hard-on that was growing just from looking at her open, sweet mouth.

I'd expected her to look like she'd been hit by a freight train. I just hadn't expected the sudden urge to pick her up, lay her across my desk, and taste every inch of her.

I leaned back in my chair. "You heard me."

No one got a marriage proposal just like that, and sure as shit not from *me.* But it was the way it had to be. I had to get married to get my dad—and the board of directors from hell —off my back. I had to keep my company.

No woman would fit the bill the way Cora did. The women I knew were more than happy to fuck their way to the top. That was the last thing this company needed after I'd *supposedly* run its reputation into the ground.

"I don't understand," Cora said, frowning at me. "Marry you?"

I nodded. "Yeah. I need you to pose as my wife."

"Pose? So we wouldn't really get married?"

I sighed. "No, we would indeed get married."

She shook her head, trying to make sense of what I was saying. I watched her as she tried to figure it out. Her eyes widened as she realized... something. And then her face changed from surprised to furious.

"Do you think this is funny?" she snapped at me. "Is this your latest stunt? Playing a joke on the awkward intern? I've already embarrassed myself with the whole toilet paper incident last night, so now you want to take this a step further and see what it will take to break me? Is that it?"

Her anger was a surprise. I'd expected her to be shocked, not angry.

"I'm not making fun of you, Cora," I said. "I'm serious."

Cora shook her head and stood. "I can't believe this," she said, more to herself than to me. "I figured you were too good to be true, you know that? God, I'm a fool."

I watched her, baffled.

"I have to go," she said.

Her shoulders slumped as she walked to the door.

"Don't leave," I said.

She looked over her shoulder and laughed sarcastically. "I'm sure as hell not staying. This is crazy!"

She reached for the door. I'd have to turn up the pressure a notch. I'd prepared for this scenario, even though blackmail was the last thing I wanted to do to someone like Cora.

But my neck was on the line.

"If you go, I'm going to have to report you to HR for theft. And I might have to get the police involved."

She stiffened when I said that, her hand frozen on the

doorknob. For a moment, she didn't move. Then, she slowly turned around.

"I thought you said it didn't matter," she said softly.

I sighed. She looked so hurt. As if I'd betrayed her. And she barely knew me.

"I know what I said," I answered her. "But that was yesterday, before I learned I'm about to lose my company. You can walk out of here, but I'll have you fired for theft. Or... you can marry me."

She narrowed her eyes at me. "That's a very unfair ultimatum."

"Yeah," I said gruffly. "I know. Trust me, I'm in the same boat as you."

"I highly doubt that," she said icily.

I shook my head and gestured to the armchair for her to sit down again. "Let me tell you what it will mean."

She hesitated, but I knew I had her. I wasn't *really* going to fire her—I wasn't a heartless piece of shit, and I knew she was already in a bad spot with money. But she didn't know I was bluffing, and that was all that mattered.

When she walked to the armchair and sat down, she perched on the edge, knees pressed together, hands folded in her lap. She was tense. That smile I liked was gone.

That was my fault.

"I need to save face with the board of directors. They're upset about my public behavior and the image I'm giving the company."

"I don't blame them," she said tightly.

I glared at her before continuing.

"You need my help here as much as I need yours, so I wouldn't get too arrogant about it," I said. "I need you to be my wife—legally—and play the part for six months."

"Why only six?" she asked.

For someone who was between a rock and a hard place, she had a hell of a lot to say.

"I need you to stick around until my probationary period is over. When I became CEO, I began a year-long probation with the board of directors. I've got six months more until I'm home free." I'd done a bit of reading. I knew my contract forward and backward now, and neither Dad nor Allison Evans was going to catch me with a loophole again. "During the next six months, you'll live with me rent free, I'll cover all your bills, and when it's all over... I'll pay you three million dollars."

She gasped when I mentioned the money.

"Three million... are you kidding me?"

I shook my head. "I've never been more serious about anything in my life. There is a catch, though."

She narrowed her eyes. "Oh?"

"You have to play your role well enough that it convinces the board of directors to let me keep the company."

"Oh," she pouted.

"That's a fair deal for three million, don't you think?"

"Yes, I think so." She paused, and I could see her working through everything I'd said. I didn't quite know what that sum of money meant to her—money wasn't the same to me as it was to everyone else. But I knew she needed cash, and I was willing to bet that three million was more than enough for her.

She frowned, and I wondered if she was going to take me up on the deal. It was a lot of money, but being married to a stranger for six months... God, I didn't even know if *I* could do it. I wasn't the marrying type. I was a free spirit. I didn't want to play happy family. But if I wanted the company, I had to do this.

And despite my father's angry words, I *did* want the company.

"We'll get a nice and tidy divorce at the end of it," I said breezily. "You'll have your own room in my apartment. You'll live comfortably. And don't worry, you won't have to sleep with me."

Her eyes darted away, and her face turned bright red.

"Unless you want to," I added.

Her blush deepened. She stifled a cough as she shifted in her seat.

"Of course, you'll need to make appearances as my wife," I continued. "Play the part and all. A kiss or two might be called for. And neither of us will be able to date anyone else during this time."

She threw me a doubtful look.

"Rest assured, I'm completely capable of restraining myself, Cora."

"Three million?" she asked quietly.

"Three million."

"I'll do it," Cora said, and it was my turn to be surprised. "That was easy."

"No, I'm not done," Cora said. "I'll do it, but I have conditions of my own."

"You're not in a position to make demands," I said.

"The way I see it, neither are you," she pointed out. "Or should I step back and let you find someone else to marry?"

I grunted. She wasn't stupid—she had to know that the women I usually hung out with weren't marriage material, not even for an act.

"Or even better," she pressed on. "I could go to the media and expose you for attempting blackmail and a sham marriage. The board would can you on the spot."

Ouch. She was tougher than she looked.

"Fine," I said. "What is it?"

"If I'm going to be living with you, I need you to take care of my mom's living expenses, too. And you need to hire a housekeeper and a nurse who can look after her when I'm not there. Someone who will cook and clean and make sure she's okay. She can't be left all alone. Consider it an advance on the three million."

It seemed fair. More than fair. And selfless. Cora really was something else.

"Okay," I agreed. "It's a deal."

"And not later, Bryce," she said, her eyes fierce. "I need you to make those arrangements right now."

Fuck, her ferocity was a turn-on. I wanted to grab her and kiss her.

But first, I had to figure out how to make this feisty woman my fake wife.

CHAPTER 5

CORA

I walked back to my cubicle, reeling. My head spun with everything that had just happened. This morning, I'd left my house panicked that I wouldn't be able to keep a roof over my head. Now, I was engaged. Sort of.

It didn't really count as an engagement—the arrangement between me and Bryce was more of a business transaction. But still, I was suddenly to be married.

When I reached my desk, I sat down and closed my eyes. I focused on my breathing, the way it traveled in through my nasal passages when I inhaled and out through my mouth when I exhaled. In, out. In, out.

"Are you okay?" Avery asked.

I opened my eyes and started nodding, but suddenly, tears sprang into my eyes.

"Oh, honey," Avery said, looking worried. "What's wrong?"

"I can't talk about it here," I said.

Avery glanced in both directions before she answered. "Dana will have our heads if we sneak off now, but as soon as it's lunchtime, we're going to grab something outside the office and you can tell me all about it."

I nodded. I wasn't sure if I could tell Avery. But she'd struck me as trustworthy from the first moment I met her. And I had to get it off my chest. I couldn't talk to anyone else about it.

Especially not my mom. I knew what she would say if I told her that I'd just agreed to be someone's wife for a shit-ton of money. She would tell me that no matter how bad things got, it wasn't ever *that* bad. But she was wrong.

Things really had gotten *that* bad, and I wasn't going to let us be out on the streets. I hadn't been able to get it right for my mom. We were drowning in bills, and the house was about to be foreclosed on.

This was my way out.

It wasn't exactly what I'd hoped for when I'd wished something big would happen—I'd had something like getting a new job in mind rather than getting married. But this was what the universe had given me.

When lunchtime rolled around, Avery and I fled the office. She insisted on going to a trendy coffee shop, though I wanted a cheaper place. Like a saint, she offered to pay for our food when I told her I was tight on cash.

Soon, I'd have more cash than I knew what to do with, and I could make it up to all the people who'd helped me out.

"Okay, spill it," Avery said when we sat at the Fresh Roast Bistro two blocks away from the office. "What's going on with you?"

I started telling her what had happened, how I'd let the bills slip because I hadn't been able to cover them all, how I'd stolen toilet paper—a new low—and how Bryce had given me money.

"He's so dreamy," Avery said with stars in her eyes.

I snorted. "It gets better."

I told her the rest of the story—the foreclosure on the house, and Bryce's demand that we get married. After I told her the whole thing, she blinked at me, her mouth open.

"Yeah, I didn't know what to say either," I said.

"Cora, this is insane," Avery said. "Are you serious? You want to do this?"

I sighed. "I don't have much of a choice. I mean, what's the alternative? Not only will I get fired for stealing, but my mom and I will be out on the street and there's no way she'll be okay if we don't have a home. She's getting better but it's a slow process. I can't do that to her, Ave."

Avery nodded slowly. "You're the most selfless person I know."

"Stop," I said, feeling silly. "You would have done the same for your mom, too."

Avery nodded. "Yeah, I guess so. But this is big, Cora. Although... I doubt it'll be too awful to be around Bryce Hollis all day. Oh, my God, the guy is a dreamboat."

I giggled and shook my head. "Yeah, he's dreamy all right. But it's not how I ever imagined Prince Charming would sweep me off my feet. He's not even interested in me. Just what I can do for his image."

"Wait. Do you think he'll back out and not give you the money?" Avery asked.

I blinked at her. "I hadn't thought about that. Surely, Bryce would stick to his word?"

"You better get it in writing. Just like any business deal. After all, that's exactly what this is."

I thought about it. "I don't know if this is a business deal that we can put on paper," I said. "I think it might jeopardize what he's trying to do if there's any proof of what it really is."

"Yeah, I guess so," Avery said. "Just... you know, be careful."

I nodded. I was going to get married to someone for

money. This wasn't about love. As long as Bryce kept his word—and I suspected that he would—there wasn't much that could go wrong.

I just had to be sure I kept my heart out of the equation. Which I didn't expect to be an issue. I was under no illusions about what this marriage meant.

No matter how gorgeous Bryce was, and how nice he could be sometimes, he was a player who used women to get what he wanted. He was using me, too. Just not in the same way.

But then again, he *had* hinted that his bedroom door would be open...

"What if he wants me to sleep with him?" I asked.

"Why wouldn't you want to sleep with him?" Avery asked. "God, every woman in the world wants that, and you're going to have access to him twenty-four-seven. You're the luckiest person I know."

I tried to see it that way, but Bryce wasn't the love of my life. I wasn't planning on spending the rest of my life with him.

I was still a virgin because I'd never dated a guy special enough to be my first. I didn't expect that would change with Bryce.

No matter how dreamy he was.

I was grateful for Avery taking me away from the office for lunch. By the time we returned to our desks, I felt a lot better. And determined to make it work somehow.

It was for my mother's sake, if nothing else.

An hour later, Bryce summoned me to see him again. It irritated me—would I have to jump every time he snapped his fingers?

"I have work I need to do," I told him when I walked into his office. "You can't keep calling me away from my desk. If

Dana thinks I'm a slacker, she's not going to give me the job I need."

"Don't worry about Dana right now," Bryce said, taking his blazer from the coat rack and shrugging into it. "You're coming with me."

"Where are we going?"

"Home."

I frowned as I followed Bryce to the elevators.

Home?

I struggled to keep pace with him as he quickly walked outside to the parking lot, stopping at his Maserati, and opening the door for me. He drove me silently through the city, stopping at a luxurious building with a doorman. At last, we walked through the doors of his enormous penthouse.

I gasped.

My eyes first swept over the waterfall in the foyer then moved toward the expansive view of the ocean through the windows. My mouth dropped as I took in the marble floors and ornate furniture. My head spun. Everything was incredible. It smacked of money.

So this is how someone like Bryce Hollis lives.

"This is going to be your home, and I want you to be comfortable," Bryce said when he gave me the tour. "I want you to feel like what's mine is yours. Nothing here is off limits to you, do you understand?"

I nodded, looking around, gaping at the marble statues in every corner and oil paintings on the walls. Priceless finishes and state-of-the-art technology that combined to make the penthouse apartment fit for one of those magazines where they celebrated luxury condos.

Being in his home, everything started to feel real.

This was happening. We were actually getting married, and I'd spend six months in this luxury apartment.

"When are we supposed to do it?" I asked, turning to

Bryce when we stood in front of the large windows in one of the guest bedrooms that looked out over the ocean. "When are we getting married?"

"As soon as possible without it being suspicious. Right now, the board knows I'm single, so we're going to have to fool them into thinking this happened for real."

I raised my eyebrows. "That sounds impossible. No one falls in love overnight."

"What are you talking about? Romeo and Juliet's love affair happened over the span of three days."

"And look how it ended for them."

Bryce laughed. It was a good laugh, as if he didn't have a care in the world. "We'll figure it out."

I took a deep breath and tried to let go of the tension on the exhale.

"We're just going to sign a piece of paper, right? Then it's done? Almost like eloping."

Bryce looked grim when he shook his head. "I'm afraid it's not going to be that simple. We're going to have to do the whole thing—a big party with the dress and the cake and the guests. To make it look real."

My jaw dropped as I stared at him. "Are you serious?"

He nodded. "Yeah, I am. Our next stop is the best wedding coordinator in the city. You're going to work with her until you have the wedding of your dreams. You get to have it all, everything you've ever dreamed of since you were a little girl." He smiled as if it was supposed to excite me.

I felt like I'd been hit by a ton of bricks, and I sank into the armchair by the window to catch my breath.

I didn't know how to tell him that I'd never dreamed of weddings when I was a little girl. My mom had taught me from an early age that fairy tales never came true. She'd drilled into my head that I needed to stand on my own two feet rather than rely on any man to take care of me. It was ironic that I was doing just that—getting married to a man so that he could pay the bills. But it wasn't the same thing.

Okay, so maybe I *had* dreamed of getting married once or twice when I was younger. But I'd always thought I'd marry someone I was in a relationship with, someone I loved.

But there was no time for sentimentality. I had to keep my eyes on the prize.

"Ready?" Bryce asked.

"For what?"

"To go meet the wedding planner."

I nodded. "I guess so." Even though I wasn't remotely ready at all.

The rest of the afternoon was spent talking to the wedding coordinator. The woman was a shark. She looked the part—she had dark blonde hair styled perfectly, makeup that made her look like she'd stepped from the cover of a magazine, and she was eloquent, selling the Big Day as something every woman would want. She almost got me excited about the idea... until her entire team arrived, everyone a bride might need to plan a wedding.

And I was bombarded with questions. What color scheme did I have in mind? What kind of cake did I prefer? What would our menu be? What music would the DJ play? They asked me so many questions, I felt like the Spanish Inquisition had time traveled to twenty-first century Los Angeles.

And the more they interrogated, the more swatches they threw at me, made me taste cakes and talk about different heel heights, the more panicked I became.

My throat closed and I struggled to breathe. I was pretty sure I was on the verge of an anxiety attack. But the team kept pushing for more.

Bryce stood to the side, not offering any input at all. He made one call after another, pausing only to type out emails on his phone.

And finally, I couldn't take it anymore.

I turned and stormed away, leaving the showroom to hide in the ladies' room down the hall. Locking myself in a stall, I gave in to sobs that racked my body. The stress and sudden upheaval in my life was too much for me.

A few minutes later, I heard a knock on the door.

"Go away!" I cried out. I wasn't ready to face the wedding coordinator or any of her team members. I wanted my mom here. Or Avery. I wanted someone who gave a damn about my feelings and what this would mean for me. I was doing a very big thing, and for all the wrong reasons.

"It's me," Bryce's voice sounded through the stall door, and I blinked.

"What are you doing in the ladies' room?" I asked.

"Come on, Cora," he said. "Open up. Talk to me."

I opened the stall door, not even worrying that the bit of makeup I wore had smudged around my eyes in dark circles that made me look like a raccoon.

"What's wrong?" Bryce asked.

"Are you kidding me?" I asked. "Do you not know the answer to that question?"

I hiccupped. Bryce reached for me and rubbed his hands along my arms. It sent electricity through my body for him to touch me like that.

"Talk to me," he said. "We're in this together, you know."

"No, we're not," I said, new tears running onto my already wet cheeks. "You're standing over there doing nothing at all while I have to give her all these answers for a wedding I didn't even know I was having until this morning. It's too much, Bryce. I haven't even wrapped my mind around the fact that I'm getting married yet, and we're already talking about butterscotch filling."

Bryce nodded. "You're right. I'm sorry."

I frowned. "Really?"

"Yeah. This is a big deal. And I'm not being as involved as I could be. I'll change that."

"Are you being serious?" I asked, narrowing my eyes at him. For someone who didn't seem to care about me beyond what he could get out of this arrangement, that was a considerate thing to say.

"Yeah," he said. "I am serious. I know it's not easy, and I'm asking you to do something very big. So… what can I do to help?"

I thought about it. This wasn't just about the dress and the cake and the decorations and the menu. It was about so much more—about my mom not being here, about everything I'd been taught as a little girl, about the fact that we'd been surviving alone all these years without a man to help us.

I needed to not be so alone in this crazy pretend world.

"I want something real," I said. "I don't want it all to be fake."

"Something real," Bryce echoed.

I nodded. "Yeah. I want…" I thought about it for a moment. "I want to meet your family. And I want you to meet my mother. This can't just be about business, not if it's going to be for six months."

Bryce hesitated. "It's just me and my dad," he said. "My mom left when I was very young. So, there's not much of a family to meet. But if meeting my grouchy old dad is what you need, then we'll do it."

I blinked at Bryce and suddenly, I saw him in a different light. He was an only child, just like me. And he only had one parent, just like me. I wouldn't have thought we had anything in common, especially not that Bryce came from a broken home, too. But maybe there was more to Bryce than met the eye.

Maybe I didn't know him at all.

"Thank you," I finally said.

"For what?"

"Meeting me halfway."

He nodded. "It's the least I can do, Cora."

The way he said my name sent a shiver down my spine. But I could think about *that* later.

The important thing was that he was polite and sweet and willing to give me what I needed. I had no idea what I'd expected from Bryce during this whole process, but it wasn't this.

Maybe, somehow, I could get through this wedding—if we just took it one step at a time. And if I didn't think too hard about what I was about to do.

If I overthought it, I'd have another panic attack, and that wouldn't do.

Six months, I told myself. That was all. In the grand scheme of things, it was nothing. And since Bryce would take care of my mortgage issues and my mom's medical bills, my burden was already lightening.

Now, I just had to accept the truth, no matter how startling it was.

I was marrying a stranger.

CHAPTER 6

BRYCE

*C*onvincing my dad to get on board was harder than expected.

When I told him I was marrying a respectable woman to please the board of directors, he didn't think I was serious.

He thought I was fucking with him because I was pissed off about Allison. But I told him everything—how I'd just met Cora, and how she'd agreed to the plan. We were indeed getting married. His disbelief soon gave way to shock.

After the shock wore off, he was worried.

I couldn't remember when last I'd seen my dad this worried about anything. His life had always been simple enough. He'd worked himself to the bone to build the company, and that had been admirable. I couldn't remember a day when money was an issue—we always had more than we needed. My dad never seemed to think spending time with me was that important. He'd been okay with letting nannies raise me. He seemed to take life in stride.

But now, this marriage thing had rattled him.

I sent him my research findings on Cora. I'd run complete

background checks on her, even hired an investigator to do the job properly.

The girl had an impeccable history. A GPA of 3.9 from a respectable university on scholarship, well-rounded extracurriculars and glowing letters of recommendation when she'd applied for her internship. Not so much as a speeding ticket in her life. My instinct had been spot-on about her—she was squeaky clean. Stealing two rolls of toilet paper had probably been the only dishonest move she'd made in her life.

That had satisfied my dad a little. Cora's wholesome image would work wonders for the publicity of the company.

I'd also put Allison Evans to work. She'd convinced the gossip website that broke the story on my weekend with the three models to run a correction and a public apology. Now they claimed their information had been outdated. The website promised their readers that my crazy weekend had *actually* happened months ago.

As far as all the tabloids were concerned, Bryce Hollis was officially a one-woman man. Today, a flurry of articles had appeared speculating about who the lucky woman was.

The PR spin had come out perfectly. Maybe this would work after all.

But when I arrived at my dad's house this evening, he looked worried again.

"What's wrong, Dad?" I asked while we waited at his mansion for Cora and her mother to arrive.

It was the meet-and-greet dinner. Cora and her mother, me and my dad—everyone was meeting each other for the first time.

"I don't know if this is a good idea," my dad said. "I get what you're doing, and it's good to see you so serious about the company, but it's crazy. And I don't know if you're going to be able to pull this off. If she's not completely committed…"

"She's going to be fine," I assured him. "She's got more than enough reason to make this work."

"Yeah, the bribe," my dad grumbled.

"It's not a bribe, it's a business deal," I pointed out.

"Sure," my dad huffed, not convinced in the slightest.

I was nervous about meeting Cora's mom. My dad knew this whole thing was a façade, but Cora had asked me not to tell her mom that it wasn't real. She said that her mom wouldn't understand, and that after she'd been through so much, she wouldn't be able to handle it if she thought her daughter was getting married for anything other than love.

It was already a hard pill to swallow that everything was happening so soon.

We'd rehearsed our official story—the one we'd tell Cora's mom, as well as the board of directors. We'd met at work, fallen madly in love, and had decided to make it easier on each other and HR by getting married.

It wasn't foolproof, but a lot of people married on impulse. Besides, no one would be able to prove otherwise. Who was anyone to judge young love, after all?

I'd promised Dad that Cora was a capable actress, that he was worrying for nothing.

But, deep down, I worried that I would end up losing the company after all.

But one thing at a time. First, the dinner.

I was surprised to realize that I wanted her mom's respect. I wanted her to think that I was worthy of her daughter's time and affection. Even if that affection was just pretend.

When they arrived, I didn't allow the butler to receive them. Instead, I walked to the front door myself.

Cora was helping her mom out of the car.

What I saw when the older woman came to me was nothing like what I'd expected. She was thin and frail, looking like a stiff breeze could blow her away. It was clear she'd been very sick for a very long time, and my heart constricted for Cora's sake. Things had to have been tough at home.

But when I was introduced to Rachel Rhodes, her eyes were an intense steel gray. There was no doubt that the woman underneath that paper-thin skin was tough as nails.

I hoped that wasn't a bad sign.

"Ms. Rhodes, it's wonderful to meet you," I said, holding out my hand.

"None of this," she said and weakly pulled me closer. I allowed her to hug me. "And call me Rachel, please. I don't like being called Ms. Rhodes. It feels so formal."

I nodded and smiled before I turned to Cora and kissed her hello. It was just a chaste peck on the lips, but it was more than we'd ever done. In fact, we'd barely been in each other's personal space except for bumping into each other.

Her eyes widened a tiny bit in surprise at the intimate gesture, but she didn't show her shock in any other way. We were supposed to be intimate around each other, and we had to convince Rachel that we were engaged.

The whole thing was backward. I would have to fix that soon—I wanted to kiss Cora like I meant it. I wanted to give her a toe-curling kiss that left her breathless, to do it right if this was what we were going to do. But that would have to wait for later. We had a show to put on.

"Dad," I said, turning to my father. "This is Cora."

My dad held out a hand and Cora took it. "It's so nice to finally meet you, sir," she said. "I've heard great things about you. Of course, not only from Bryce, but in the news, too."

"Call me Sal," my dad said right away. "And the media

exaggerates a lot of things. I'm not the man the newspapers make me out to be."

Yeah right, old man, I thought to myself.

His words sent me reeling. Dad was a giant in the business world. Everyone revered him, if they didn't fear him.

His public image—the great Sal Hollis—*was* the real him. He was my father. I should have known him better than anyone, right?

My thoughts turned bitter, but I pushed them away. There wasn't time to dwell on that.

After my dad and Rachel were introduced to each other— and he said something under his breath that made her blush a wild red—I suggested we take the party inside.

"You have a beautiful home, Sal," Cora said when we stepped into the house. She looked up at the Moorish columns and carved ceilings, and her eyes went wide.

"Stunning," Rachel added.

The house was very different from my penthouse in the city. It was a large estate in Malibu with incredible ocean views and classic Spanish architecture.

"Thank you," my dad said, looking around. "I have to admit I haven't spent a lot of time here until recently."

"It's a shame," Rachel added. "I wouldn't leave the house if I lived in a place like this."

What my dad didn't mention was that I grew up on this estate alone, with the best tutors, nannies, and au pairs a boy could ask for. But my dad had never been here. His office had been his home.

My office, now.

We walked to the dining room where everything was prepared for our guests. Cora and I sat next to each other, with my dad at the head of table, and Rachel across from Cora. I took a deep breath—so far, so good. Rachel and my dad were a little uptight, but the circumstances were unique.

"This looks lovely," Rachel said when the first course was served. It was a cucumber and cream summer soup. She sipped a spoonful and nearly turned green at the gills.

"Are you okay, Mom?" Cora asked, worried. She'd been watching her mom like a hawk. It wasn't hard to tell that Cora had been a caregiver for the older woman.

"The soup is delicious. It's just a bit rich," Rachel said, looking apologetic. "I haven't been able to stomach anything too fancy over the last couple of months."

I jumped up. "Don't you worry about that. I'll have them bring you something simpler."

"Oh no, please—" Cora started but I wasn't going to let her stop me. The point was to impress. I knew Rachel was in ill health, and I wanted to make sure she was taken care of.

In the kitchen, Carl, the chef, was chopping onions. He looked up, shocked that I'd walked into his domain.

"Put together a light salad," I ordered. "No spices or dressing, keep it very simple. Get it out to me as soon as you can."

Carl nodded and I left the kitchen, walking back to the dining room.

I stood next to Rachel and reached for the soup to remove it. My arm grazed the glass of water she'd poured herself and it fell over, spilling its contents onto the tablecloth and over the edge of the table.

Fuck!

"Oh!" Cora cried out, jumping up at the same time Rachel pushed her chair back. Half of the water had spilled onto her lap, and her clothes were damp.

"I'm so sorry," I said, offering her a napkin.

She pressed it against her pants and shook her head with a smile. "It was an accident, Bryce. No need to apologize."

I felt like an idiot for spilling a glass of water in the woman's lap when she was already not doing very well. I shook my head in dismay at my bad move.

Cora fussed over her mom, and my dad watched them with an unreadable expression on his face. When it was clear there was nothing more I could do, I sat down in my seat and sipped soup from my spoon, feeling like a fool.

When Cora sat down, and the chef had replaced the soup with a light salad, Rachel ate. I was glad that was working, at least. But the rest of the meal was going to be problematic. I had asked Carl to prepare veal, and there was nothing plain and simple about it.

I jumped up and ran back to the kitchen, asking Carl to prepare a simple stew in broth for Rachel, with plain rice to go with it.

"I don't understand," Carl said when I put in my request.

"The rest of the food will be thoroughly enjoyed by the three of us, but there are dietary requirements I wasn't aware of. And I'm not paying you to question me."

Carl sighed and nodded, jumping to it.

When I returned to the dining room, I was relieved to see smiles on everyone's faces, rather than the scowls I'd somehow expected. I couldn't say the evening was going well, but at least it didn't seem to be a complete disaster.

While we ate, my dad made small talk. He asked Cora about her experience at the company and about her long-term plans. Cora answered all his questions politely.

I groaned. "Dad, it's like you're interviewing her," I said.

My dad shrugged. "I'm just getting to know her. That's the point of this whole thing, isn't it?"

I couldn't argue with him. I studied Cora's face and she didn't seem too uptight, but I didn't really know her well enough to know how she was feeling—to be able to read her.

"So, how did you two meet?" Rachel asked when the plates had been cleared and we waited for the second course.

I glanced at Cora. *Here goes nothing,* her eyes seemed to say.

"At the office," Cora said and smiled. "It was actually so silly." She went on to explain how we ran into each other in the hallway with file folders flying. That part had all been true.

"It sounds very sweet," Rachel finally said.

Cora shrugged. "Yes, but the downside was that it made me extra late delivering the files to my supervisor. I'm pretty sure she's still upset about how late I was. And no doubt she'll hold it against me when it comes time for performance reviews."

"I'll make sure no one worries about that too much," I said. I squeezed Cora's hand where she rested it on the table.

She glanced at me and smiled warmly, and something passed between us. Something... amicable. We were in this together, after all. And in that moment, it felt like we were a team.

"The second I saw your daughter, I knew there was something wonderful about her. Something special," I said, trying to embellish the story a little. "I always thought the whole thing about love at first sight was a cliché, but in that moment, I knew it was real. It happened for me when I laid eyes on Cora."

Cora gave me a smile for her mother's benefit. But I could tell from her blush that she was a bit uncomfortable with my words.

Her mother smiled at us. "How lovely."

I met my dad's gaze but quickly looked away. It was true that I had seen something special in Cora. But I hadn't fallen in love with her like in the movies, and I hated lying to Rachel.

This would all be worth it in the end, though—for everyone.

The butler and servants arrived with the second course, and Rachel was served her stew while the rest of us had veal, roasted vegetables, and wild rice with an exotic spicy sauce.

"Thank you for making the extra effort for me," Rachel said. "I didn't want to be a bother."

I shook my head at the same time my dad did.

"It's not a problem at all," I said.

"That's what I pay the cook for. So there's no need to worry," my dad added.

I nodded and Rachel smiled, tasting her stew. "It's perfect," she remarked graciously. When she glanced up at me again, it felt like those steely eyes bore into my soul.

"So, marriage is a big step," she said, looking from me to Cora and back again. "Huge. Are you sure you're ready for this?"

I glanced at Cora and took her hand, nodding.

"Yeah, I know this is all fast. But I think we're ready," Cora answered.

"You think?" Rachel asked, narrowing her eyes.

Cora took a bite of her food so that she couldn't answer right away, stalling for time.

"What she means," I said, speaking for Cora, "is that no matter how sure people are, marriage is always a big step and no one can know what the future holds."

"So, you think there's a chance it might fail?" Rachel asked with a frown.

"That came out wrong," I said and then cleared my throat. "I'll do what it takes to make it work. And I know Cora feels the same. And if both people are trying, actively working on a marriage, I don't see how it can fail."

"Hmm," Rachel said and took another bite thoughtfully.

I glanced at my dad. He'd been fretting about the whole thing, but he was supportive. He wanted me to succeed in the business, of course. I knew he wasn't very happy about the way I was doing it, but he'd resigned himself to the fact that I marched to the beat of a different drummer. At least, this time, I was doing something to help the company's reputation.

"How did you know you wanted to get married?" Rachel asked.

God, this woman was serious about making sure we were doing the right thing. It was endearing to know that she wanted Cora to be happy, but it wasn't an easy question.

I glanced at Cora. "Well," I said to Rachel before breaking eye contact with Cora, "what we feel for each other is so strong, there's no reason to wait. I knew from the moment I saw her that this was what I wanted." I glanced at Cora again, and she was blushing.

It was sweet to see Cora blush like that. And beautiful—God, she was incredibly beautiful. But I was worried about her mother's line of questioning. Was she onto us? Did she know what we were doing here?

"There's no rush for the two of you to tie the knot," Rachel said. "You have plenty of time to get to know each other. Do you know her favorite color?"

"Mom," Cora interrupted. "That's not fair. What does my favorite color have to do with the fact that Bryce makes me happy?"

"I'm just saying I don't see why the two of you need to get married so soon. There's no reason you can't take the time to really get to know each other, date, see if this is really the good fit you think it is. If you rush into something, you can't look at it from different angles and decide if the choice is the right one for your future. It's not a pair of pants you're buying that you can exchange when you're not happy. This is marriage."

I glanced at my dad, who nodded in agreement before he looked at me.

"I think Rachel speaks very wise words."

I blinked at him. Why was he siding with Rachel? He knew how serious this was, how important it was that I married to keep the investors happy and keep the company going.

"Mom, I know what I want," Cora said. "And this is it."

"I just don't want you to get hurt," Rachel said. "And this… it seems like a dangerous game to play." She looked at me. "But you're used to playing games, aren't you?"

CHAPTER 7

"*M*om!" I cried out.

I was mortified by her quip about Bryce playing games. She was right, of course. She'd seen the articles about him, no doubt. They were everywhere. And since my mom wasn't working, she kept herself busy by browsing the internet.

"No, no," Bryce said, putting his hand on mine. "I've got this." He took a deep breath and faced my mom. "I know that I've made bad decisions in the past. But when I met Cora, everything changed. I guess that's when I realized I wanted to settle down. Because she makes me see life differently. She's got the kind of stability I never had in relationships before, and where the others didn't challenge me or excite me, I'm completely mesmerized by your daughter. I know I've made mistakes, but I know what I want now. It's all become crystal clear."

My mom studied Bryce, and I waited for her to tell him his words weren't good enough.

I knew what she was worried about. I knew she panicked about me getting married. It didn't even have as much to do with the time frame as the fact that I was getting married at all. By springing it on her the way I had, I'd raised her hackles.

And why shouldn't she be suspicious? My dad had walked out on her when she was pregnant with me, and she never saw him again. They'd known each other well before getting married, she'd said. They'd dated for two years. And she still hadn't expected him to do that to her.

How much worse could it be when I didn't know Bryce at all?

A part of me hated that I was doing this to her. I was getting married for convenience and money, not love.

But it was for my mom, for her survival.

Besides, I didn't think about marriage and love the way other women did. I'd been raised in a home where I understood the reality of love—it hurt more than anything else.

As long as Bryce and I could pull this off, everything would be okay. I was going to bounce back after these six months. I wouldn't suffer through heartbreak the way Mom had.

If anything, this pretend marriage was preferable to the real thing. By keeping my heart out of the mix, I wouldn't get hurt.

She just didn't know that. I couldn't tell her what was really happening, not yet. She would worry about the pretend marriage even more than she worried now, and I didn't want to cause her extra stress.

But as much as I hated lying to my mom, we needed a roof over our heads. If this was what it took to make that happen, then I was going to do it.

The rest of the dinner went smoother. My mom seemed to relax a little after Bryce made it clear that he was serious about making it work. But she still seemed uneasy.

One thing was clear: Bryce and I still had some details to iron out.

After dinner, I took my mom home. I made sure she was settled in for the night before I left to visit Bryce at his penthouse.

When Bryce opened the door, he was happy to see me. He didn't kiss me hello again, and I was relieved. I wasn't sure how to act around him, what would be expected of me, but it was good to know that when we were in private, he wasn't going to expect anything from me that I wasn't ready to give.

It was one less thing to worry about.

When we sat in the living room, each with a glass of wine, Bryce looked at me. His expression was serious.

"We might have underestimated what this is going to take," he said.

I nodded. "I was thinking that, too."

"It's going to take a lot more work to really convince people. A lot of people marry on impulse, but this is next level. Everyone is going to be suspicious."

He was right. They were going to be suspicious of us and why we were doing this, especially the people Bryce needed to impress. They were going to watch him a lot more closely than my mom was watching me. Bryce had to make it work for a reason. Although I was getting something out of this deal, I was just along for the ride.

"How are we going to pull this off?" I asked, taking a sip of my wine. We hadn't had anything to drink at dinner, and it felt good to let loose a little.

"I've been thinking about that," Bryce said. "And I think a good start is getting to know each other better."

I nodded. That made sense. My mom had asked Bryce what my favorite color was. It was such a trivial thing when it came to the depth of a real relationship, but most people in serious relationships knew details about each other. That was what love was, wasn't it? It was finding out the small things.

"Okay," I said. "Let's get into it, then."

Bryce grinned and fired off a bunch of questions. Favorite colors, favorite foods, favorite places to go. We offered our answers one by one and even took notes to review later. But it was going to be hard—real marriage shouldn't feel like a test, and this did. Except it was worse than a test in school. This would affect the rest of our lives.

Lives that would be spent apart, of course.

"When you were a child, what did you want to do when you grew up?" I asked Bryce after we'd lapsed into a moment of silence.

"I was always supposed to take over from my dad," he said. "I was groomed to be CEO."

"Wasn't there something you wanted to do instead, at any point?"

He paused. "I don't know. I never really thought about it in concrete terms. I wanted to get away, to have my own freedom. As a child, that looked a lot like running away, at first." I stilled when he said it but didn't interrupt. "And later, it looked like traveling. Which I did for a while, until it got old. We don't really understand what's important when we're kids, do we?"

"So, traveling the world wasn't all it's cracked up to be," I said softly.

Bryce smiled at me. "Not for me. But I'm happy here."

He sounded so sad when he said it, and it tugged at my heartstrings. Even though Bryce Hollis was a man who had everything, I wondered if he really was as happy as he claimed he was.

"What about you?" he asked. "What were your dreams?"

I smiled, thinking back to the little girl I used to be. "I wanted to become a teacher," I said.

Bryce laughed. "Of all things."

I nodded, giggling. The wine had made me feel light and carefree. "I had a great teacher when I started school and I loved going to school so much, I figured that one day, I could make other people feel that way."

"That's very sweet," Bryce said.

I shrugged. "It's like you said, we don't really get what it's about when we're kids."

When Bryce didn't ask anything else, I kept talking.

"I actually got a degree in graphic design. I wanted to get involved in marketing, but not on the back end. I wanted to be the one to create the images, to create the art."

Bryce raised his eyebrows. "You're an intern for a very different part of the job."

I nodded. "Yeah, I know. It was all I could find, though. And I needed money. Fast. I figured it would be easier to work my way up in a good firm rather than working in a small company and never being able to go anywhere. My mom needs me."

"Do you mind me asking what's wrong with your mom?" Bryce asked.

I shook my head. "Breast cancer. She's in remission now, but for a while, it didn't look like the chemo was working. I had to say my goodbyes. We were preparing for the worst. And then suddenly, it all turned around, and now I'm getting more years with her."

"You've been through a lot," Bryce said.

I nodded. "Which is why we have to make this thing work, no matter what. I'm going to see it through no matter what the others think we're doing, because you deserve that company of yours, so you can have your freedom, and I need to keep a roof over my mother's head."

Bryce smiled and nodded. "We'll figure it out."

We sat in silence for a while as the darkness of the night

wrapped itself around us. The lights in the living room were dim, and we looked out the windows over a sleeping LA.

I became aware of how close Bryce was to me. I looked up at him, and when he turned his head, his face was inches away from mine. His eyes slid over my features, and they were dark and intense.

When he lifted his hand and brushed my hair out of my face, my breath caught in my throat.

"You're beautiful, Cora," he said softly.

My stomach erupted in butterflies, and Bryce leaned in. His lips brushed against mine, and when he kissed me, warmth filled my body. He kissed me as if he meant it, as if he really liked me.

God, he was good.

Was this how he kissed all his women? Was this how he made them feel? If it was, I understood why they were all so crazy about him.

He did this with everyone.

I just had to keep reminding myself of that. This was a game, an act, a means to an end. It wasn't real, no matter how good it felt.

Bryce and I were doing this to achieve something. This wasn't a boy-meets-girl romance. It was a business transaction.

I couldn't forget that and let myself get swept up in his deep blue eyes. I couldn't accidentally fall for a man who would never return the sentiment.

That was much too dangerous.

When he broke the kiss, my heart sank to feel him pull away again. But my brain knew it was better this way.

He smiled at me, and I smiled back uneasily.

Just pretend, I told myself.

CHAPTER 8

CORA

*I*t was the day of the wedding. My wedding.

I stood in the bridal suite, in front of a full-length mirror, and I didn't recognize the fairy-tale princess that stared back at me.

My wedding dress was beautiful. It was a vision of lace and silk, with a low neckline and lace sleeves. Pearls were added to the bodice and sleeves, giving the dress a regal feel. The dress was fitted around my body, only spreading out lightly from my knees into a mermaid cut.

The veil that had been pinned onto my updo came down to the back of my thighs, and the heels were decorated with the same lace and pearls.

"Oh, honey," my mom said with tears in her eyes as she looked at my reflection over my shoulder. "You're beautiful. And you're positively glowing."

I turned around and hugged my mom. I didn't know why she'd said I was glowing—I was a nervous wreck. My stomach was twisted into a knot of nerves.

What if I couldn't pull this off? I'd only had two weeks to throw this wedding together. What if I failed and we didn't make it? What if they guessed it was all just one big ruse? But Mom seemed to believe it. I'd managed to convince her, to win her over. As long as I had her support, I would figure this out.

I knew I could. It was all for her, anyway.

Avery was my maid of honor. I didn't have a lot of friends —I'd worked too hard when I looked after my mother to keep many friendships—and the two other women in my entourage were friends from college I'd kept in touch with. But the wedding party was complete, and it was going to look good for the guests and in the photos.

I was in a daze. I went through the motions, doing what was expected of me. It felt like I was watching the whole thing from afar, as if someone else was doing this, not me.

We left the bridal suite and rode the elevator to the lobby of the hotel, where one of the rooms had been transformed into a chapel. There were five hundred guests inside, watching, waiting.

"Smile," Avery said, standing in front of me and giving me my bouquet. "It's your wedding day and you're the luckiest girl on Earth! I can't think of one woman who wouldn't want to be you."

She gave me a wink. We'd both agreed not to discuss the very fake nature of this wedding in public. I couldn't risk the truth getting out.

I forced a smile. "You're right. I can't tell you how much it means to me that you're here."

Avery grinned. "I wouldn't miss this wedding for the world. It's not every day you see a millionaire playboy committing to someone—my best friend, no less."

Avery hugged me carefully so she didn't mess up my dress, hair, and makeup, and then she smiled broadly, modeling what I should do.

The music started and she turned around, waiting for the

other girls to walk down the aisle one by one before it was her turn. And then it was mine.

"Are you ready?" Mom asked, standing by my side. She was going to walk me down the aisle, the way my dad should have if he hadn't been a piece of shit and left us. When I'd asked my mom, she'd cried.

"Ready," I said, even though I wasn't ready at all, and we started walking down the aisle.

Five hundred faces were turned to me, all of them staring at the woman Bryce Hollis had chosen as his wife. I felt sick to my stomach, almost paralyzed with terror at what I was about to do. And a pang of guilt shot through my chest because I was lying to my mom about it. But it was better this way.

I turned my head to the front and looked for Bryce. He stood next to the priest, looking at me with tenderness, and when our eyes locked, all doubts slipped away. The fear subsided, and the people faded to the background. All I could see was Bryce, the man who would get me through this. The man I was going to do this with. We were going to figure it out.

Together.

We weren't marrying for love, but we were teammates, and that was something. We were in this thing together, and it felt good to know I wasn't completely alone.

When we reached the front, my mom handed me to Bryce and she kissed him on the cheek.

"Take care of my baby girl," she said to him.

Bryce nodded solemnly. "I will," he said. He turned his eyes to me, and in them, I could see he meant it. He was going to make sure this worked out.

I was filled with a sense of reassurance, and warmth spread through my veins.

It's just an act, I reminded myself.

But damn it, he was so good at it.

I barely heard a word the priest said. After a lengthy sermon about the sanctity of marriage, and standard vows that Bryce and I had decided on together—we were going to break them in six months, so it was pointless writing our own—the 'I do's' followed, and Bryce slipped a diamond ring onto my finger.

Finally, the words came: "You may kiss the bride."

Bryce stepped closer to me and pulled me tightly against him. When his lips landed on mine, I knew what to expect—it wasn't the first time we'd kissed. It wasn't the first time butterflies erupted and I felt weak at the knees, either.

I couldn't fall for this man. No matter what I did, that wasn't an option. It couldn't be if I wanted to keep myself safe.

When Bryce broke the kiss, he looked at me with eyes that were filled with an emotion I wasn't sure how to interpret.

We turned to face the crowd, and camera lights flashed—lights that belonged to paparazzi, not only the wedding photographer. I tensed up, suddenly feeling like I was on display.

"Smile," Bryce said softly. "They just want to know who you are. Something for the front page. You've got this."

I smiled, just as he'd said, and I looked around.

Finally, we were ushered away from the crowd, and for a moment, we were alone before we would be whisked away once more for photos.

I let out a breath I hadn't known I'd been holding.

"That was crazy," I said.

Bryce nodded. "It was. But you did great."

I was glad he thought I'd done well, at least.

"Now what?" I asked. "Is there something that's expected of me?"

Bryce nodded. "You're my newly wedded wife. We're going to walk into the reception room later, and everyone's going to find out who you are and what you are to me. You just keep doing what you've been doing so far, and you'll be fine."

I nodded and swallowed hard. Bryce was at my side, and as long as we did this together, I was going to be okay.

I looked up at him and he looked incredibly handsome, dressed in his tuxedo, glancing around, ready for action. When he'd kissed me, I'd felt something… different. Something more than what I'd expected to feel. This whole thing was a farce. So why did I want Bryce to kiss me again? Why did I want more than just a kiss?

I was definitely not supposed to have real feelings for him.

The photographer appeared and beckoned for us to follow, and Bryce and I did as we were told.

By the time we returned, the guests were all in the reception room, having drinks and talking. Bryce and I were announced as Mr. and Mrs. Hollis, and the words sounded foreign. But when we stepped into the room, Bryce took my hand, and I couldn't help but smile. The way he held onto me was protective, possessive.

I liked it.

I sized up the crowd. It was a mixture of reporters and photographers from different magazines and tabloids with curious faces and nosy questions, and uptight businessmen with serious expressions that made me nervous.

The only thing that everyone seemed to have in common was wanting to know who I was and where I'd suddenly come from when Bryce and his antics had been well known for the longest time.

Every time someone asked something to that effect, Bryce was ready with an answer. I stood by his side, his fingers interlinked with mine, and listened to the way he painted pictures with mere words and somehow answered all the questions without saying anything at all. He'd been born to play this role, born to live this life. I felt a little out of place.

But the more time I spent with Bryce, the more I watched how he handled things and saw how he protected me against the press and his business associates, the more I liked him.

When everyone was dancing, and Bryce was charming a few businessmen, I snuck away to have a moment alone with a glass of champagne by the bar. I wasn't used to alcohol, and the bubbly went straight to my head. It was a relief—I was buzzed just enough not to be too worried.

"You're radiant," a familiar voice said.

I looked up and nearly dropped my glass in surprise.

My supervisor, Dana, was grinning at me. I didn't think she'd ever cracked a smile my way before.

"Am I?" I asked. "The cameras are making me nervous."

"You're really serious about Mr. Hollis, aren't you?" she asked, slurring her words a bit.

Well, well. Dana was a little drunk.

"I wouldn't have married him if I wasn't," I said, giving her the vague kind of answer everyone had been getting tonight.

"I'll be honest with you, Cora," Dana said, glancing at Bryce. "When I heard about your engagement, I didn't think you two could possibly be serious. I mean, the guy is the catch of the century. Who wouldn't jump at the chance? But the way you look at him…"

"How do I look at him?" I asked, alarmed.

"Like he really means a lot to you. Not many people look at each other the way the two of you do."

I swallowed. I wasn't sure what *that* meant.

"I'm just so happy for you," Dana said. "I know I'm not the

easiest person to work for, but you're a sweet kid. You deserve to be happy."

And then she hugged me. I could hardly believe it.

But Dana was right. I did feel something for Bryce. I wasn't supposed to feel anything, so I was in trouble. But he was just such a nice guy. The tabloids always made him sound like he used people, but the Bryce I was starting to see just wasn't like that.

This whole thing had become a lot more difficult than I'd thought it would be. When I'd agreed to this, I'd thought it was going to be simple. Get in, help Bryce, get the money, get out. Straightforward.

But it wasn't just a matter of convincing everyone that we'd fallen in love. And things were growing complicated by the second.

If I didn't play my cards right, I might just fall in love with him.

CHAPTER 9

BRYCE

The wedding was exactly what it was supposed to be—the press was out in full force, the event was spectacular, and the guests were all happy.

My dad was satisfied, and even the directors and investors seemed to have a good time.

Which meant I was over the moon.

It had all gone just as I'd hoped, and if the rest of the marriage went the way I needed it to, my future in the company was going to be cemented. I would be in the CEO chair for a long, long time.

Cora was incredible. Of all the things I had planned and worked out to a tee, she was an unexpected twist. She'd done everything I expected of her. She showed up looking like a vision in a white dress that made me want to peel it off her right then and there, she'd been graceful during the cere-mony, and at the reception she'd smiled and laughed.

She was perfect.

She'd led everyone to believe she was the whole package, the real deal. She'd given them a glimpse of why I wanted her to be my 'forever,' just as I needed them to believe.

And something told me that the way she'd been acting hadn't been an act, per se. She'd been herself in a lot of ways.

And that had opened something inside of me, too. It made me feel... nice. It was something other than lust. The wedding was romantic, and I'd been swept up in it all. When I'd looked at her and said, 'I do,' I'd almost convinced myself I meant it.

Now, after the biggest part of the night was over, I leaned against the bar and looked out at the dancing couples. Cora was with her friends in the corner, talking and laughing and having a good time.

My head spun a little—I'd had a lot of champagne. And whiskey. And shooters. My groomsmen, all friends of mine from way back, had kept buying me alcohol at the bar. Who was I to say no when my friends wanted to spoil me on my wedding day?

The one day I didn't have to pick up the tab myself.

And fuck, I'd needed the alcohol. I'd needed to let loose. Because my head was spinning, and not just with the alcohol that flowed through my veins. Cora was in the middle of it all, the center point that seemed to keep everything else from spinning out completely.

And all of this... the wedding and the vows and getting dressed up... it had to mean something, right?

I'd never given a shit about marriage. The whole concept of picking one person to love, only to lose them in heart-break or—even worse—to make each other miserable for the rest of our lives, had always seemed pathetic to me. Marriage was an archaic convention that lost its merit centuries ago. I had always been a firm believer that not all animals mated for life, and that included humans. We just weren't wired that way.

It was why the divorce rate was so high, why so many

people cheated. We just weren't meant to stick with one person for so long.

I'd made a good run of hopping from one partner to the next. I'd practically turned it into a sport.

And yet... when I looked at Cora, I felt a pang in my chest. My head spun a little more. I had no idea how I'd ended up in this situation. I was married. *Married.* Just thinking about it made me break out in a cold sweat.

And at the same time, I felt calm and collected because I knew exactly what I was doing.

Maybe the panic was the alcohol talking. I'd had too much to drink. I should have cut back. I should have stayed on top of shit. Because when I was sober, I knew exactly what I was doing, and I was calculated and cool about it.

Now, I didn't feel calm at all. I looked around at everyone who had come to the wedding—there were a lot of beautiful people here. People who moved in high circles. The investors' wives were all prancing around, hoping they'd outdressed each other. The paparazzi kept flashing their cameras, angling to get the photo that would bring their story to the front page.

And even though these people were familiar, I felt oddly removed from them all.

They were all here for the event of the year—the marriage of the biggest playboy in LA. It wasn't every day something like this happened, after all. It wasn't every day that a wealthy player settled down with... well, who exactly was Cora to me? Who was she to the rest of the world? What would they call her in the tabloids come tomorrow morning when the rest of the world wanted to find out exactly what had gone down within these walls?

Would they call her the girl next door? Maybe they'd portray her as a trap I'd fallen into, making it seem like she'd caught me for my money. Or she'd be cast as a saint—the woman who finally got me to settle down.

I had no idea what they would do. And for the first time, it bugged me.

Not what they were going to say about me—I never gave a shit what they said about me, which was why we were here in the first place—but what they were going to say about her.

If they tore her apart in the tabloids… the idea got me hot under the collar. I threw back the whiskey I'd been sipping on.

Why did I give a shit? This whole thing was a sham. But when she kissed me at the end of the ceremony, it felt *real*.

I wanted more.

And now, I couldn't stop staring at her. Even though I knew we were just playing pretend. Even though Cora wasn't the type of girl I ever went for. Even though all of this was fake.

Finally, the night wrapped up. The guests left, and we were on our way out, too. Cora called to make sure her mother was safe at home—the caregiver I'd arranged had moved in two days ago. Now that we were on our way home, Cora was quiet, looking out at the city sliding by as we were driven to my apartment.

We weren't going on a honeymoon. It wasn't a good time to be away from the office. I didn't trust the board of directors for a second.

"Are you okay?" I asked, reaching for Cora and brushing my fingers along her arm.

She glanced at me and nodded. "It's just a lot to take in."

"It is," I agreed. "But tonight went well. You did great. Thank you."

She blinked at me, surprised. "You're thanking me?"

I nodded. "This is a big deal, you know. And I know what it takes for you to be here, with me and not with your mom."

Cora sighed. "It's hard to be away from her. I keep think-ing, 'what if she's not okay, what if she needs me?'"

"She's in good hands. And if she needs you, we can get there in a flash."

Cora nodded and looked out of the window again. I wished I could help her feel better. And that—the fact that I wished stuff like that—was what fucked me up. Because I wasn't supposed to be so invested. Not when this whole thing was a game, a business deal.

When we got to the penthouse, I flicked on the lights until all the darkness was driven away. I turned to Cora. She smiled at me, but it was awkward. I stepped a little closer to her and took her hands in mine. The atmosphere shifted a little. She seemed to defrost, and the worst of the awkward-ness bled away.

"After all the acting and the faces we had to put on, I'm glad you're here," I said.

"Really?" she asked.

I nodded. "I know this is just a business deal between us, but I like spending time with you, Cora. And we took a huge step today. Everyone seemed to be happy. So far, so good."

"I guess so," she said with a smile.

God, she had a beautiful smile.

I hooked a flyaway strand of hair behind her ear and looked into her eyes. She swallowed, and her gaze slid to my lips for just a moment.

She wanted to kiss me.

I wanted to kiss her, too. Then, I wanted to take her to my room, unwrap her, and have her in every way possible.

I was getting ahead of myself. I wanted *her* to want all that, too.

But fuck, I wanted her so badly. My cock was hard in my pants. I looked into her big eyes, letting my gaze drift down to her perfect lips, her curvy body. I'd been dreaming about this since that day in the hallway.

I was a guy with needs. And I needed her.

"So, we should probably consummate this thing, huh?" I chuckled. I'd meant it as a joke, to break the tension, but Cora's eyes widened. I'd terrified the poor girl.

"I was just kidding," I quickly said. "I mean, we talked about this. I'm not going to pressure you."

"It's not that," Cora said and swallowed hard. She glanced away. "It's just…" She took a deep breath and turned to face me again. "I'm a virgin." She said it quickly and let out a gush of breath afterward.

"What?" I asked, frowning.

How was that possible? How could someone as beautiful as Cora still be a virgin? In this day and age… I doubted I knew anyone who was even close to being a virgin.

"I just haven't… you know. I've been waiting. For the right guy."

I blinked at her, struggling to believe what she was saying. She'd waited? She'd saved herself? I suddenly had even more respect for her than ever. To not give yourself over to temptation because of something bigger and deeper than physical need… I couldn't believe it.

"I'm sorry," she said softly.

"No," I said, shaking my head. "Don't ever be sorry for that." I took a step away from her. So help me, I wasn't going to try to seduce her. This was different.

This was Cora.

"Come," I said, turning away from her and leading her to the main bedroom. I stepped a little closer to her again. I kissed her gently on the lips—a chaste kiss, no tongue—and stepped away again.

"If you need anything, I'll be next door."

"You're sleeping in a different room?" she asked.

I nodded. "Yeah. That was part of the deal, remember?"

"Okay," she said and nodded, too.

"Sleep well, beautiful," I said.

She blushed lightly. "You too."

I pulled the door shut behind me and walked to one of the guest bedrooms, dropping myself on the bed. God, of all the things I'd ever done in the world... passing up an opportunity wasn't one of them. But I wanted to do right by her. I wasn't going to pressure her into doing something she wasn't ready for. Especially if it was her first time.

Even though I wanted more than anything to taste her sweet virgin pussy.

I sat up and started stripping my clothes off, climbing under the covers naked and alone.

But the truth was, I wasn't truly alone anymore, was I?

No, I was married now.

I wasn't sure if I should feel horrified or thrilled.

CHAPTER 10

CORA

*W*hen I opened my eyes, sun streamed into the large main bedroom through open curtains. Last night, I hadn't bothered closing them. The lights of the city had been beautiful, and when I'd tried to close the curtains and close my eyes, the room started closing in on me. I'd felt like I was going to spiral into a panic attack.

Leaving the curtains open had soothed me, and I'd fallen asleep staring at the twinkling lights of the city far below me.

Now, the room was bright and beautiful. A haze hung over the city that made it look almost magical.

I was in a large poster bed, the feather down covers all around me soft and puffy, and the sheets were probably a thousand thread count.

And I was completely alone.

This wasn't how it was supposed to be on the morning after my wedding. I should have been wrapped in the arms of the man I loved, tangled together after a night of *not* sleeping, where we came together as one.

But this was nothing like that.

Bryce wasn't the love of my life, and I hadn't been ready

to get in bed with a stranger—although we knew each other a little—after a marriage that wasn't real except on paper and in photographs.

I stared up at the beamed ceiling, and last night slowly came back to me. The wedding truly had been a beautiful event, and despite what we were doing, I'd enjoyed myself. That was, after the stress and panic had subsided a little. I'd had a good time with my friends from college and my co-workers, and it had been eye-opening to see how Bryce behaved himself in front of the press and his colleagues. He was clearly someone who was used to being in the spotlight. In fact, I had a feeling he loved being watched.

But even though he'd put on a happy face for everyone around us, he hadn't once made me feel like it was a one-man show. He never treated me like an afterthought. All the way through, he'd made sure that I was okay. He'd held my hand, he'd checked me, he'd been loving and affectionate.

I groaned inwardly. That had been an act, too. Right? It had to have been. We had to convince everyone that this was real so that he could keep his job.

When we got home last night, I'd been a lot tipsier than I'd let on. There were gaps in my memory this morning.

But I hadn't forgotten how gallant he had been last night.

We'd nearly kissed, and I would have let him do a lot more, even if I wasn't ready for it. I'd had too much to drink, and his confident masculinity was a turn-on.

Bryce was intoxicating even when I didn't have a drop of alcohol in my system.

But he'd pulled away, and he'd told me he was going to sleep in a different room. He'd treated me with respect that seemed very out of place for a man who was supposed to be a womanizer. I'd read all those articles—I loved celebrity scandals. Bryce had been the center of attention so many times, every time with a new woman on his arm. I'd always thought of him as a womanizing ass, someone who didn't care at all about the women he was with.

But after how he treated me last night…

I didn't know what was real. Was it real that he'd cared enough to allow me space? Or was that part of the act?

Bryce was the whole package—he was incredibly handsome, rich, and impossibly charming. He was the CEO of a large company, and his future was bright. That was what everyone said about him, and I agreed on all those counts.

But he was also a player. He didn't go out with beautiful women so he could tuck them into bed and then go sleep alone.

All of this with me… it was *fake.*

I couldn't let myself get swept up in an illusion. The point of the whole marriage was to put on an act. I needed to keep my head straight. My emotions had no place here.

I was doing it for money, he was doing it for his company. Neither of those things allowed for anything like love.

No matter how good he made me feel. No matter how many butterflies I got when he touched me, or how much of a gentleman he was pretending to be.

It was all for show.

I only had to get through six months with him. That was it—how hard could it be to co-exist with someone for six months before moving on with the rest of my life?

I preferred not to try to answer that question. Instead, I climbed out of bed, brushed my teeth and my hair, and left the main bedroom in search of Bryce so we could get this show on the road.

After walking through the entire penthouse—and it was huge—I couldn't find Bryce anywhere. For some reason, I'd thought he would be up and at 'em already. But finally, I found him in one of the guest bedrooms, still snoring away. His hair stuck up in little tufts, and he was buried under blankets and pillows. I smiled and turned to leave. My elbow knocked against the door, and I winced.

"Cora?" Bryce asked in a thick voice.

"I'm so sorry," I said. "I was just leaving."

"Don't leave," he said, holding out his arm, beckoning to me. "Stay."

I swallowed and nodded, moving closer. When I sat carefully on the bed, Bryce wrapped his arm around my waist and pulled me against him so that I lay on top of the puffy covers, his body pressed against mine.

Heat washed through me as he sleepily nuzzled my neck. Goosebumps ran over my arms. This felt good.

"Did you sleep okay?" he asked.

I nodded. "Yeah, just fine. Your bed's amazing. You?"

"I'm hungover as fuck," he mumbled.

I couldn't help myself. I giggled.

"What?" he asked, peeking at me through one eye.

"You're just so…"

"What?" he asked, frowning through both eyes now, lifting his head.

"Human," I said.

He dropped his head on the pillow again and groaned.

"Yeah, I'm not immortal, or I wouldn't feel like I'm fucking dying."

I giggled again. Bryce *had* seemed immortal, so far removed from the rest of the world in his tabloid kingdom. But he was a guy with a hangover, squinting in the harsh light of the morning sun that fell straight into his window. I noticed his curtains weren't drawn either, and I wondered if he'd looked out over the city the same way I had last night.

"Tell me something," Bryce mumbled.

"Like what?" I asked.

"I don't know. Anything. I want to get to know you. Tell me… about your past. Your boyfriends."

I hesitated. "I don't have much of a dating history," I admitted. It was nothing like his, but I didn't say that out loud. "I've been in two serious relationships before…"

"Before this," he finished the sentence for me.

I nodded and smiled. "I guess this isn't exactly serious."

"Well, it's not just for shits and giggles," Bryce said, and for some reason, that made me burst out laughing. He chuckled as I giggled about what he'd said, and when the giggles died down, I sighed.

"I'm still trying to wrap my mind around it all," I confessed.

"Yeah, me too," Bryce said.

I blinked at him. For some reason, I'd figured he was just taking it in his stride. But seeing him like this, hungover and honest, opened my eyes to a very different man.

"So, two serious relationships," Bryce encouraged.

"Yeah," I said. "They weren't right for me, though. I just always felt like something was missing. I want to be with someone who completes me, and both those relationships felt like hard work."

"That doesn't sound right," Bryce agreed.

"Yeah… it's why I didn't sleep with them. Or with… anyone." I glanced at Bryce to gauge his reaction, but his face was expressionless, his eyes curious as he listened to what I had to say.

"I just feel like it should be special, you know? Not just the next step because it's expected."

Bryce nodded. "That's really noble, Cora."

"Really?" I asked.

For some reason, I'd expected him to think it pathetic. I hadn't thought that someone like him—who slept with women the way other people breathed—would understand something like that. But he wasn't mocking me when I studied his face. His eyes were serious. He truly thought it was a good thing.

"Thank you," I whispered. "The thing is…"

I hesitated, not sure how to put this.

"What?" Bryce asked.

"Well…" I took a deep breath. "I don't know if I feel like that anymore."

"What do you mean?" Bryce asked, frowning.

"I think I've been making too much of a big deal out of it. I mean, yeah, the first time should be a good experience, but maybe it doesn't have to be as *perfect* as I've made it out to be."

I glanced at Bryce, who didn't look like he understood what I was saying.

"I'm attracted to you, Bryce," I said. "And I want to do that. With you."

I could hardly believe what I was saying.

But it was true. I did want to sleep with him. Desperately. All my big talk earlier about keeping my emotions out of this arrangement—well, I could have sex with him and still do that, right?

His bulging, muscular arm felt so good around my waist. His scent was intoxicating. I wanted all of him.

"Are you sure?" Bryce asked, but his features had already changed. His eyes had become deep, filled with hunger, and his lips were slightly parted.

I nodded. "Yeah. I mean, I know I want this with you. But it's my first time…"

"I'll be careful," he said gently, running his fingers lightly down my cheek. "And the moment you want to stop, you tell me and we'll stop, no questions asked. Okay?"

I nodded. "Okay," I said in a breathy voice. God, could he be any more perfect right now?

He pulled me closer to him, so that our bodies were

pressed against each other, and through the thick cover, I could feel his erection. He kissed me, and my body came alive as his tongue slid into my mouth.

He didn't taste like last night's alcohol or morning breath or anything awful. He tasted fresh and *delicious*. And the way he kissed me made me melt.

Bryce's hand slid down my neck, slowly dragging his way to my shoulder, where he thumbed my collarbone, and then onto my chest, the delicate skin of my breast. When he cupped my breast through the thin nightgown I wore, my nipple was erect.

He massaged my breast as he kissed me, and I moaned into his mouth. He was doing something so small, but it was turning me on like crazy. My head spun, my nerve endings felt alive, and my body was on fire.

Bryce rolled over, pinning me down, and the weight of his body on mine was incredible. The covers were half-folded over me now, and when I ran my hands down his sides, I froze.

"You're naked," I whispered.

Bryce chuckled against my mouth. "Yeah, I prefer to sleep naked."

He kissed me again, grinding his hips against me so that his erection pushed against my crotch through the covers. I ran my hands down his body and onto his ass, squeezing.

God, he had a perfect ass. Holy shit.

When I moaned, he smiled.

"You moan a lot," he said.

"I can't help it."

"Don't try." He nibbled on my lip. "It's fucking hot."

Bryce lifted himself off me and flipped the covers off the bed so that we were on the mattress with no covers in sight. I stared at him in his naked glory.

I had always known he was hot—everyone knew that

from the photos that were posted of him—but *God*. He had chiseled abs with tan, flawless skin, and his blond hair and piercing blue eyes just made him look so incredibly hot I could drool.

His huge cock was erect, straining, and the tip glistened with need.

I reached for him and wrapped my fingers around his shaft, sitting up.

He sucked in air through his teeth when I touched him, and I started pumping my hand up and down. He groaned.

"You're fucking good at that," he said.

I smiled at him. "I said I was a virgin; I didn't say I haven't fooled around a little."

His eyes darkened, and he leaned forward, kissing me. While he kissed me, he started tugging up my short nightgown. There was a moment where we had to come away from each other so he could get the flimsy material over my head, but the second it was off me, we came together again, his lips locking on mine and my hand finding his cock.

While I rubbed him into a frenzy—judging by how shaky his breathing became—his hands found my breasts, and he rolled my erect nipples between his thumbs and forefingers. I moaned as it sent jolts of electricity right down to my sex and I got wetter than I'd ever been before.

Bryce carefully pushed me backward so that I lay on my back. He started kissing his way down my neck, onto my chest, and then his cock was too far away to reach.

"Just feel," he said, and I closed my eyes and gave myself over to the sensation.

His mouth closed around my right nipple, his hand still massaging and kneading the other breast as he licked and sucked, and I moaned and curled my body beneath him.

When he moved over to the other side, he repeated his process, and I was just about dying for him to be inside of me. I had never been fucked, but my body knew what it wanted, and I ached for him in a way I'd never ached for anyone.

Bryce lifted his head to my face again, kissing me while he slid his hand down my body, over my stomach, and between my legs. I gasped when he pushed his fingers into my wetness, slowly exploring me. When he moved his fingers to my clit, rubbing in circles, my gasps and moans changed.

Judging by the way he looked at me, his face riddled with amusement and lust, what he saw and heard was a good thing.

I was glad about that—I couldn't help but show how much I was enjoying it, and holy *fuck,* the way he touched me and kissed me was incredible.

I wanted to know what it would be like if he was down there with his mouth. I'd had that before, but Bryce was something else. Nothing I'd done before had been the way it was with him, now.

Bryce didn't move, though. He didn't change anything except his pace, and an orgasm started building inside of me. I moaned and cried out as the heat at my core built more and more until it was so powerful, it felt like it was going to rip me apart. When I orgasmed, I came undone at the seams. I cried out and moaned, bucking my hips against his hand.

When I came down from my sexual high, Bryce grabbed a condom from the nightstand and put it on his length. He gently rolled on top of me. He lifted himself onto his arms, planted firmly on either side of my head, and his eyes locked on mine.

"I'll be gentle," he promised. "But there might be some pain. Tell me if you need me to stop, okay?"

I nodded and he pushed his cock against my entrance. I held my breath in anticipation and when he slid into me, I cried out. A sharp, stabbing pain washed through my body but only for a second before pleasure followed straight on its heels.

"Are you okay?" Bryce asked, concern all over his face.

I nodded. "Keep going," I gasped.

He slid further into me, deeper and deeper, until he was buried all the way inside of me. His hips were flush against mine, my legs splayed wide, and he lowered his face and kissed me as I got used to the incredible feeling of having him inside of me.

I wanted more.

CHAPTER 11

BRYCE

I'd fucked a lot of women in my life but never had it felt so perfect as when I slid into Cora. She was tight—tighter than anything—but she was so fucking wet, it made everything perfect.

When she cried out, I worried I'd hurt her too much, but then she begged me to keep going, and damned if I was going to say no to that. She felt *fantastic* around my cock, her body clamping down around my shaft, as if she wanted to pull me in deeper than I could go.

When I was buried to the hilt, I kissed her. I wanted to let loose and fuck her for all I was worth, but she deserved for it to be done right. So, instead of ramming into her again and again, giving in to my primal urges, I held back and kissed her, focusing on the feel of her body under me, around my cock, the taste of her lips on mine and her tongue as I swirled mine around her mouth.

She moaned and gasped, and holy shit, the sounds she made were such a turn-on. She was a shy person, but between the sheets—holy fuck—she wasn't shy about letting me know how she felt at all.

After a moment of pause where I just let her get used to the idea of having me inside of her, I pulled back. I slid out of her almost all the way so that only my tip was buried before I slid back into her. *Slowly*, I told myself. Slowly.

She moaned softly as I slid into her again, and her chest rose and fell with her erratic breathing.

"Are you good?" I asked her. I wanted to keep checking in with her. Under no circumstances did I want this to be a bad experience for her.

"Oh, fuck yes," she breathed.

I chuckled, surprised by the expletive.

"Don't stop," she added.

And who was I to turn down a pretty girl when she asked me so nicely?

I pulled out again and pushed into her. And again and again, picking up pace. The harder I pushed into her, the louder she cried out.

"Cora?" I asked.

"Stop checking if I'm fine and fuck me, Bryce!" she cried out. "Harder!"

I laughed and did as she asked. She was on board with this whole thing, fine with it, much quicker than I'd thought she'd be.

I started pounding into her, fucking her harder and harder, listening to the symphony of her moans and cries. She gripped my shoulders, her fingers digging into my skin, and it was so fucking hot, I had to concentrate not to lose my load right away. But there was no way in hell I was finishing so soon. I was going to ride this one out for as long as I could.

I didn't want to stop. Ever.

After a few more thrusts, Cora's breathing changed, and I could tell she was building up to another orgasm. The first one had been so damn hot, it had taken all my self-control to not just slam into her there and then.

This time, when she came undone, she curled her body around mine, her nails biting into my skin. She cried out loudly before she closed her eyes and her mouth was open in a silent cry of pleasure. I felt her pussy contract around my cock, her body pulsating with waves of pleasure, and again I had to focus on not coming. I had to breathe through my balls tightening. It took every ounce of my self-control not to lose it right there and empty myself inside of her.

But I wasn't done, yet. I wanted more.

When she came back to me, fluttering her eyes open and gasping for breath, her face filled with the delirium that followed a great orgasm, I planted a quick kiss on her parted lips.

"Get on top of me," I said. "That way, you control it."

I pulled out of her, and she whimpered in protest. When I lay on my back, she clambered onto me. Her skin was slick with sweat, and the flush that spread over a woman's body when she was well and truly turned on colored her breasts and her cheeks and her pussy.

When she lowered herself onto me, I guided my cock to her entrance, and when she sat down, we both groaned. Her eyes rolled back and her long blonde hair hung over shoulders. I reached up to her perfect breasts and squeezed them before I put my hands on her hips.

Slowly, I guided her back and forth, helping her ride my cock, showing her how to slide it in and out of her. She was a quick study. She started rocking back and forth, her natural instinct taking over. She parted her lips and gasped as she bucked her hips a few times. Her eyes locked on mine, and she leaned forward, her hands on my chest as she started bucking her hips back and forth, faster, and faster.

I groaned, holding onto her hips, pulling her farther

forward and pushing her farther back than she could go herself, and the feeling of her riding me was pure ecstasy.

"Oh, God," she cried out. "I'm going to come again."

"Do it," I gasped.

She rode me harder and harder, working up her orgasm. Her gasping turned into little moans as her breathing became so shallow I doubted she was getting much oxygen at all. But it didn't matter to her. Her eyes were shut, and the orgasmic expression on her features was hot as hell. When she orgasmed, it was even more intense than the first time. She cried out sharply, and I felt the pleasure roll through it.

She collapsed onto my chest, riding out the wave of ecstasy as it shook her, and I starting pumping into her from beneath. I fucked her, holding her tightly and bucking my hips as hard and fast as I could.

My balls tightened, and a moment later, I released inside of her with a sharp cry of my own.

She was still orgasming, and the two of us rode out the pleasure together, letting it roll over us like waves.

I didn't know how long we were caught in this pure bliss. When it finally subsided, Cora collapsed completely on top of me. I wrapped my arms around her and held her tightly as her heart hammered against my chest, and together, we relearned how to breathe.

I couldn't remember the last time I'd had sex that meant anything more than getting off. I fucked women because I needed the release, and I got a kick out of being able to get whoever I wanted. But with Cora, everything was different.

Even the sex. It hadn't just been hot as hell, it had been sensual, and we'd been connected in a way I'd never felt with someone before.

It was damn close to what I imagined 'making love' to be like. It couldn't be love, though—we barely knew each other, and we definitely hadn't done any of this because we cared about each other and wanted to spend the rest of our lives together.

Right?

Why did everything feel so incredibly perfect with her, then?

After our mind-blowing sex, we lay together in my guest bedroom. I'd retrieved the duvet from where I'd dumped it on the floor and pulled it over both of us. We lay facing each other, and I studied her features. I couldn't read her expression.

"Are you okay?" I asked.

She nodded and a smile spread over her features. "More than okay. That was bigger than anything I could have imagined."

"What was bigger?" I asked. If she was referring to my cock, well, that would be a hell of an ego stroke. But I knew she didn't mean that.

"Everything... the emotions, for one. And what it all felt like. The intimacy... I'm not explaining myself very well."

I shook my head. "Don't worry. I think I get it."

She nodded and smiled at me again, and her smile was beautiful. She was beautiful—everything about her was genuine and straightforward. It wasn't just physical beauty, either. The more I got to know her, the more I realized what was inside was more incredible than what I was seeing on the outside.

There was something special about her... and it wasn't just the fact that I married her.

Cora was different. Unique. And she intrigued me. I wanted to know more. She was the first woman I wanted to stay in my bed after we fucked. And that part wasn't just because we were married, either.

"And you were bigger, too," she said, blushing. She

brushed her fingertips shyly against my cock, which caused it to stir and wake up.

"Is that so?" I asked, smiling at her.

She nodded and bit her lip. "I never knew it would feel like that. To be so… filled up."

Fuck. I was ready to go again, but I knew I'd have to take it easy on her. It had been her first time. So I changed the subject.

"So, marketing design, huh?" I asked, going back to what she'd told me before about what she wanted to be.

She laughed. "Yeah, well, things change, right?"

"You know, you can still end up doing that. You're not so far from it now."

"I know," she said. "But right now, I'm trying to do what's best for me and my mom. I don't want to chase my dreams if it means she's going to stay behind."

"That's really sweet," I said. "You're very close, you and your mom."

Cora nodded. "Yeah, it's always just been the two of us. If you're facing the world together, you need to be close. And after she got sick and I thought I was going to lose her…" She swallowed hard. "It just takes a lot—out of both of us—to fight that hard to survive and we needed each other. We leaned on each other. It sounds crazy, but she was the one that pulled me through. I don't think I would have gotten through her being so sick if she'd passed away." She laughed softly. "She says the same about me, but I don't know how true that is. I do everything I can, but between the two of us, she's the strong one, the rock."

I listened to how she spoke about it all and realized that this woman and her mother had been through so much pain together, it was no wonder that she was so different from all the others I'd met who'd had it so easy.

"Was your father not in the picture when you were growing up?" I asked carefully.

Cora shook her head. "He left when my mom was pregnant with me. I don't know where he is or what he's doing with his life. Hell, I don't even know his name."

I blinked at her. "That's got to be rough."

Cora shrugged. "It's the only life I know, so it's not as tough on me as it's been on my mom. But we got through it."

"I know what that's like," I said.

"Yeah?" Cora frowned a little.

"Yeah," I said. "My mom left when I was really young. My dad raised me and built a company, all alone. Well, not completely alone. He had nannies and stuff to help him raise me, so that part wasn't too hard on him. I mean, we're not very close or anything. But I get what you must have been through."

Cora reached for my cheek and cupped it with her hand, her eyes filled with sympathy.

"I'm sorry," she said.

I shrugged it off. "It's fine. Like you said, it's the only life I've known, so it's not too bad. But I don't want that, you know? The whole illusion of love. It just shatters."

I turned my head to her. Her face was carefully expressionless, but her eyes were still filled with emotion. And now that I was talking, I kept going.

"I just don't think I'm cut out for love, you know? I've given up on that. The women I cared about in the past were just gold diggers, and I'm not about to be used for my money."

"That's awful," Cora said softly. "Being used isn't only unfair, it's a different level of hurt."

I nodded, and we lay in silence for a while. I couldn't believe how similar we were and how much more open I felt toward her now. It was like the sex had brought down walls I hadn't known I was letting down, and I'd told her things I hadn't meant to.

But it felt good to talk about them to someone. And it was a nice feeling that she knew what it was like, and that she could relate.

Eventually I turned to face her again. "I think we need to get breakfast," I said. "And then we need to face the music."

"What music?" she asked.

"The board of directors."

Cora groaned. "I don't know if I'm ready for that."

"Hey," I said and pulled her tightly against me—I loved having her this close. "We'll figure this out together, okay?"

She nodded, and I kissed her on the forehead. I just wished I could believe those words myself.

CHAPTER 12

CORA

I was terrified.

We hadn't been married a full twenty-four hours before I got my first assignment.

My first official duty as Bryce's new wife was to impress the members of the board who wanted to get rid of him.

And I was petrified I was somehow going to screw it up.

I wasn't cut out to be any kind of important figure. I hadn't been groomed my whole life to be charming, to handle business, to say all the right things at the right times and to bring across a certain image. I was shy and reserved, used to being hidden away in a cubicle among dozens of other similar cubicles with nothing that set me apart from the rest of the working class.

And now, suddenly, I was Mrs. Hollis. I was someone that people expected things from.

I had no idea what I was doing.

The assignment to meet the board members tonight was a little unexpected. This morning, Bryce had just sprung it on me.

Now, I stood in the bedroom, getting ready for a cocktail

96

party that was being hosted at the office building.

I looked at myself in the mirror, assessing my handiwork. I wore an emerald-green cocktail dress with a scooped neckline and a formfitting shape that swished around my feet when I walked. I wore medium-height heels with it—enough height to look classy but not so much I couldn't keep my balance in them, for which I was grateful. I already had so much I needed to focus on.

I'd done my own hair and makeup. Bryce had offered to hire someone to do it for me, but having someone dress me up two days in a row was too much.

When I looked in the mirror, what I saw wasn't too shabby.

Bryce stepped into the room.

"Wow," he said, staring. "Holy shit."

I blushed bright red. "What?"

"You look fantastic," he said. "That dress was definitely the right choice."

He'd chosen it for me.

Bryce took a few steps closer, and I expected him to wrap his arm around my waist and pull me tightly against him the way he'd done earlier when we'd had breakfast together. But Bryce was already in work mode, his mind on how he was going to impress the board members, and he didn't reach for me the way I wanted him to.

"Are you ready?" he asked.

I nodded, although I wasn't ready to do this at all.

He turned and left, and I followed him out of the penthouse, down the elevator, and to a sleek black car that waited for us. We slid into the leather seats—Bryce held the door for me and climbed in after me—and the car purred to life. We drove to the office in silence. I'd hoped he would coach me on what to do and what to say, but he was silent. Maybe he was as stressed as I was.

Or maybe he wasn't stressed at all.

I'd only been to the top floor of the building a couple times. The place had been transformed. The living room—or staff room or whatever it was—had been decorated and set up as a party room. Tall cocktail tables were scattered around the edges, complete with waiters with black waist-coats and silver trays floating around, handing out hors d'oeuvres and delivering drinks from a bar that had been set up at the far end.

"Can I get you something to drink?" Bryce asked me when we stepped into the room.

"A glass of wine would be great," I said. I needed something to help me relax.

Bryce nodded and disappeared. I looked around and noticed men in suits standing around, talking. The board members, I was willing to guess. I recognized some of them from the wedding.

I tried to spot Bryce, but a waiter appeared in front of me with my glass of wine. Oh. Bryce wasn't going to bring it to me himself.

"Mrs. Hollis," someone said. I turned to face an older man wearing a suit and tie. He smiled at me, but his gaze was steely. His hair was almost completely gray, but his eyes were sharp. He held a glass of whiskey in his left hand.

"Cora, please," I said with a smile and held out my hand.

"John Morrison," he said and took my hand. His were calloused and rough. He tucked his hand into his pocket after letting go of me. "There are a lot of questions surrounding your relationship with Bryce."

I nodded. "Isn't that always what happens when people break tradition or go against convention?"

Morrison laughed. "Indeed, that's true. But tradition is what our society thrives on, and convention is the foundation of some of the largest firms in the country."

"And innovation? Intuition? Times change. Business can't always be conducted the way it used to be." I let out a breath, relieved I didn't shudder. Morrison was intimidating, and I was in the deep end, not even sure if I could swim yet.

Morrison narrowed his eyes. "Maybe not. So, what is it that you do?"

"I work for Hollis Marketing," I said. "I'm…" I'd nearly said I was an intern, but that wouldn't go down very well. "I'm interested in Marketing Design."

"Ah," Morrison said, nodding. He took a sip of his whiskey. "Convenient that you're working at the very company your husband owns."

"We wouldn't have met otherwise, so I would say so," I said.

Morrison laughed again. "You're witty. That might help you navigate this world of sharks."

I sipped my wine. I wasn't sure if he was right about that. I wasn't sure I was managing at all. It felt like I was on the verge of losing control of the conversation.

Another man joined us and introduced himself as Louis Stark. He was even older than Morrison, but he had equally sharp eyes. I was starting to think age didn't mean anything in the business world—these men were far from retiring.

"Is he bothering you?" Stark asked me.

I smiled politely. "We were just discussing the value of tradition in our modern society."

Stark snorted. "John here will try to convince you that everything is about tradition."

"Tradition is the only thing that keeps us all in line," Morrison said. "It's the structure through which success is possible."

Stark rolled his eyes. "What do you think about it?" he asked me. "Do you think that Hollis Marketing should maintain a conventional image? Well, probably not. You married Bryce."

I blinked at him. "What does that have to do with anything?"

"Well, it's no secret he's a womanizing playboy. You're the last in a long line of women, my dear," Stark said.

I cringed a little at that.

"People change," I said.

Morrison and Stark both seemed skeptical.

"No one stays the same," I insisted. "We're all changing constantly. Every cell in our bodies changes, transforms. Anyone is capable of changing their habits and personality, especially if they have great motivation."

"Like saving the company?" Morrison asked with a twinkle in his eyes.

"No, that's not what I meant," I said, but Stark and Morrison were both smiling. Shit! Had I put my foot in my mouth? Had I made things worse by saying that?

"What I'm trying to say," I said, trying to fix it, "is that it takes a life-changing event to really motivate someone. Bryce is the CEO of the company now. Maybe it's taken him a while to fully come into his own. But leadership and responsibility might just be what he needed to step up and do the right thing."

"Like getting married," Stark said.

I shook my head. This was coming out all wrong. I wasn't explaining it very well, and the more I talked, the more it sounded like Bryce being the CEO had been enough reason for him to try to cheat the system.

Bryce, like a handsome knight in shining armor, appeared at my elbow.

"Sweetheart," he said in a velvety voice. "Are these gentlemen giving you a hard time?"

I glanced at Bryce, hoping that my cry for help was

apparent in my eyes.

"We're just learning so much about Cora and how you two came to settle down together," Morrison said.

I cringed. This was going terribly.

"Well, we'll have to postpone this talk, gentlemen. I want to spend some time with my wife."

Bryce led me away, his hand gently on my elbow, and swept me into a dance to music that floated from invisible speakers. No one else was dancing, but I didn't care—Bryce had saved me. I was grateful that he'd whisked me away from those two vultures.

"Thank you," I breathed, trying to bring my emotions under control.

"I realized you were drowning with those two," Bryce said. "I'm sorry, I shouldn't have left you alone. I'm not used to having someone around that I need to look out for. I've always done these things alone."

I nodded and swallowed hard. "I think I might have ruined the whole thing." I felt like crying.

"Why?" Bryce said.

I recounted our conversation. Bryce was silent, swaying us to the music while he thought.

"We'll figure this out," he said. But his worried expression wasn't as reassuring as his words, and I had the awful sinking feeling that I'd screwed the whole thing up. We were right out of the gate, and I was already failing at the one thing I was supposed to do to help Bryce.

God, maybe it would have been better if he'd chosen one of the slinky models he was always seen in the tabloids with. Anyone other than me would have known how to handle this. I had to open my big mouth.

"Hey," Bryce said gently. "Quit worrying, it's going to be okay."

I nodded, but I wasn't so sure that it would be.

CHAPTER 13

BRYCE

When I got to the office the next morning, the board was gathered in the fucking boardroom, waiting for me.

I groaned when Terri informed me I was going to have to start the day by facing the assholes.

Before I walked in, I prepared myself. I squared my shoulders, cleared my throat, and remembered who I was.

Bryce Fucking Hollis. The CEO of the company.

Sure, I needed the board members to run the company and to keep me in a position of power, but at the end of the day, I was the CEO. I was the son of the great Sal Hollis. And they weren't going to run me off.

"Gentlemen," I said when I walked into the boardroom, walking around the large table with all the men in suits seated around it so that I stood at the head of the oval-shaped table. "What a way to start the day. What can I do for you?"

"We're here to talk about that woman you're putting on display as your wife," Morrison said right away.

I raised my eyebrows. "I'll ask you to talk about her with more respect. She's the woman I chose to marry."

"To what end?" Stark chipped in. "We're not fools, Bryce. We can see what this is all about. You're about to lose the company because of your man-whoring ways, so you grabbed the first girl that came along to make it look like you've settled down. But we're not buying it."

I rolled my eyes. "What would make you believe that I'm not in love with her? That I don't want to spend my life with her? Is there a set time for someone to be dating and then engaged before they're married? I didn't realize there were rules like that."

They all muttered and shook their heads, and Morrison snorted.

"You're not going to win this way, Bryce," he said. "It's too convenient that you got married so soon after we questioned the morality clause in your contract. And your reputation, your history, contradict this change of heart."

I was getting pissed off. Not only because they were right —I hated it when someone else was right and I was wrong— but because they couldn't know for a fact that Cora and I were doing this with an ulterior motive. They couldn't know what I did or didn't feel for her or how she felt about me.

"So, that's it, then?" I asked. "You believe it's impossible for me to fall in love, and therefore, I'm doomed. Are you so fickle that you'll believe the society pages over what I'm saying to you right now, in the flesh? Aren't you contradicting yourselves?"

They looked confused, so I pressed on.

"You claim you want the CEO to reflect traditional values. Yet here I am, married and spending every evening at home with my wife, yet you still have a problem with me."

They didn't respond, so I took the opportunity to wriggle

out of the meeting before anyone said something I couldn't answer.

"Gentlemen, if this meeting is about your lack of faith in my personal decisions, if this is about whether or not you think I have a heart, I'm not going to stand here and let you cross-examine me like I'm on trial. I know what I feel for Cora, and there is no law, no rule in the company, that stops me from getting married to the woman I love the moment I decide I want to do it. So, unless you have a better reason to take up my time, I'm going to leave this boardroom and get back to doing what I'm here to do—run the company."

I walked out of the boardroom with measured strides, hoping to God no one was going to challenge me on my speech.

No one spoke.

When I reached my office, I let out a breath and sagged into my chair. I swiveled to the large windows that over-looked the city.

Two days—two damn days. That was all it took for them to decide that they didn't believe me. Fuck them! Fuck them for wanting me out of the company, fuck them for sticking their noses in my personal business, and fuck them for thinking they could take me on about it.

I was at the top of the food chain here. I'd do my damnedest to stay at the top, too.

And they were pissing all over my parade.

Cora had apologized profusely after the cocktail party. She had been panicked that it would all fall apart. But I wasn't upset with her. Not really. It would have been better if she'd handled the conversation she'd had with Morrison and Stark differently, but that was partly my fault.

Not only had I left her to fend for herself in a room full of people who were used to being out for the kill, but she wasn't used to living this kind of life at all. I couldn't expect her to know what to do and say to make sure everything went smoothly.

I should have been there, by her side, the whole time. I had to start looking out for more than just myself.

Someone knocked on my door and marched in before I could respond. It was Morrison.

"You won't pull this off, Bryce," he threatened. "I'm going to expose you for the fraud you are. You should come clean and get it over with before you lose more than you can afford."

I shook my head, my anger bubbling to the surface.

"Who the hell do you think you are, telling me what my agenda is? I love Cora. She might not be groomed to walk into a room of board members and say just the right things. But there's no clause in my contract that requires her to do that. We're in love, and that's what matters. That's why we got married—because I couldn't imagine a life without her. And if that offends you, if that is the mark of a weak businessman and you're the one who decides it, well, by God, the larger part of the American population should be fired."

Morrison opened his mouth and closed it again without saying anything. He didn't know how to respond, and I relished that small victory. Seeing John Morrison speechless was a feat in itself.

"If you have nothing else to say, I'd like to get to work," I said.

Morrison studied me, and I had no idea what he was thinking.

"Okay," he finally said. "If you claim that you love this woman so much, I'll take your word for it."

"What?" I asked, confused that he was being reasonable. Morrison had been a lot of things during his tenure as a board member, but reasonable was seldom one of them.

"I hear what you're saying, and just because I've clawed

my way through three divorces, it doesn't mean that you can't be happy. Most of the other board members think you know what you're talking about, anyway. I'm the one who thinks you've got something to hide. But I'll give you the benefit of the doubt. Just know that the moment you fuck up, I'll be all over you like a cat on a mouse. You won't get out of it with your pretty face and your smooth talk, then."

He turned around and left my office, and I sat at my desk, gaping.

I looked out over the city again and thought about Cora. She was doing me a great favor by being my wife for six months. I'd told the board members I was serious about her. I was starting to think that maybe it was true.

The speech to convince Morrison hadn't all been lies. I did care for her. There had been a kernel of truth in my words.

Cora was special. She was different. And despite this whole marriage being a sham, an act, I liked her. She wasn't just kind and considerate and compassionate. She was also funny and smart and interesting. I didn't want to ditch her the way I had countless other women. I wanted her to stick around.

In fact, the thought of her leaving in a few months seemed awful, and I pushed it away immediately.

It was confusing as fuck, the new emotion I felt for her.

I didn't know what I felt for Cora. But I knew that I felt something.

CHAPTER 14

CORA

We were out shopping, just Bryce and me. It seemed crazy that he was coming with me to do this. And it was crazy that money was no object. For so long, I'd been used to turning over every penny before spending it, making sure again and again that it was something I could afford to do.

And here we were, walking down Rodeo Drive, and Bryce was telling me how money was no object and I could get whatever I wanted.

Whatever I wanted!

God, I wasn't even sure what that meant anymore. For so long, I'd pushed everything I wanted out of the way and put my mom's needs first. The other things—material things—hadn't mattered as long as I had her with me. As long as she was going to survive, as long as she was okay.

But now I had to focus on myself. On being okay, too. My future, and our finances, depended on me getting this right.

"I'm pretty sure I'm going to screw this up," I said to Bryce as we walked.

He glanced at me before shaking his head. "I trust you."

"Your trust is misplaced," I said. "I don't want this to go wrong, but this is *me* we're talking about. Whenever I open my mouth, all the wrong words seem to come out. And this event…"

"It's a charity gala," Bryce said.

"Right. I just know I'm going to make a mistake."

Bryce stopped and turned to me, putting his hands on my arms.

"You're going to be fine," he said. "And no matter what, we're going to get through this together."

He'd said that before.

"Come on," Bryce said. "Let's find you a dress that will make you feel invincible."

I nodded and followed him to a boutique he'd decided on.

In the store, a slew of shop assistants fussed over us, bringing dresses for me to choose from, from princess ball gowns that were so wide around me I didn't think I'd be able to fit through a door, to tightly fitted mermaid cuts, and everything in between.

While I tried on the dresses and discussed colors and shapes and cuts that were flattering, Bryce was invested and involved, telling me his opinion, joking with the assistants, and making sure that I was in good hands.

He cared.

At least, he cared about making sure that I was ready for this charity gala because he wanted to save his own ass. He cared about me because he cared about himself. It was backwards logic, but the fact that he cared about me still meant something.

I looked in the mirror at the fifth dress I'd tried on, and it was to die for. The material was a shimmery champagne color that was a modern spin on a Gatsby style, and it was light and breathable. When I moved, I didn't feel trapped like

I had in some of the other dresses. When Bryce looked at me, his eyes darkened the way they had the other night.

I knew exactly what he was thinking and blushed.

"I think this is the one," I told the shop assistant, then I walked back to the dressing rooms and slid out of the dress.

Bryce was clearly turned on by what he'd seen, and that made me feel hot and bothered, too. It had been a week, and we hadn't slept together again. Whenever I thought about that first morning together, my stomach exploded in a wave of butterflies again, and I could almost feel an echo of the orgasmic bliss that I'd experienced that day.

When I thought about it, my core tightened and I wanted it again.

But I didn't know what to expect from Bryce. I didn't know if that was something we would keep doing, or if I was just like all the other women in his life and he'd gotten what he wanted and that would be it.

I forced my thoughts to the gala.

It was a big event for Bryce—I knew how important it was, and I was worried that I would screw up. I would just have to keep my head straight, to not say anything unless it was absolutely necessary, and make sure that Bryce looked good.

That couldn't be too hard, could it?

After shopping a while longer—Bryce insisted that I get other things, too, for future events and everyday wear—we filled up the trunk of his car with new clothes and accessories.

"That was exhausting," I said.

Bryce laughed.

"What?" I felt silly that he was laughing at me.

"You're the first woman I've met that doesn't want to shop all day. And spend all my money."

I shrugged. "I'm not in the habit of buying a lot of things I don't need. And being out in stores all day long isn't my idea of fun."

"Let's do something fun, then," Bryce suggested. "There's a wine tasting at one of the local vineyards this afternoon. Do you want to go?"

"Yes!" Wine tasting sounded like a lot more fun than shopping. And I loved the impromptu idea.

We drove through the city, leaving LA and arriving at the vineyard in question. Bryce and I joined a group of high-rollers and almost-familiar minor celebrities who tasted the wines one by one and made informed exclamations about them.

The afternoon was warm, the wine was free-flowing and delicious. The tipsier I became, the more Bryce and I touched each other. I loved spending time with him. I loved being around him.

I hadn't had much time to prepare myself for what it might be like to be Mrs. Hollis, but I never thought it would be like this. I hadn't expected Bryce to be so warm and so attentive to my needs. I hadn't expected to have this much fun. When I'd agreed to marry him, I'd seen it as a six-month work contract that would be challenging but worth the time and energy it would take to get it right.

I hadn't for one moment thought that I would be enjoying myself this much, and never in my wildest dreams had I thought Bryce Hollis could be so normal, so human. He'd always seemed like a god—or a devil—of some kind. But the more we spent time together, the more I got to know him and see the side of him he only showed when we were away from the public, the more I liked what I saw.

When we got home after dinner—we'd eaten at the restaurant next to the vineyard—I was still tipsy. The alcohol had gone to my head pretty quickly and stayed there.

Bryce and I made it up to the penthouse, giggling and joking.

When we were inside the apartment, I smiled at him.

"Thank you for today," I said. "I really had a good time. I didn't expect to have that much fun."

"Me neither," Bryce admitted. "But having little adventures like that is my favorite thing to do. I hate always having everything planned. My whole life is arranged according to a schedule for the sake of the company. I had to get used to that, at first. But this..." He took my hand, his fingers interlinking with mine, "I think I can do this."

I looked up at him, and his blue eyes were bright, his pupils dilated. The atmosphere changed between us, getting thicker, more loaded, and I swallowed hard. I had to behave myself. I had to keep myself in check. This thing was still about business. Bryce wasn't in this because he was attracted to me.

Although... the way he looked at me made me think he was.

Usually, I was too shy to do anything, to act on my feelings. But I had alcohol running through my veins, and it gave me liquid courage. Before I could think about it too much—my logical, responsible mind had switched off a while ago, anyway—I stood on my toes and kissed Bryce.

He was surprised for just a moment before his arms wrapped around my waist and he pulled me tightly against him.

He tasted like wine. I was shy, but the alcohol in my body egged me on to act on what I felt.

Which was aroused. I wanted him with every fiber of my being.

He matched my urgency, kissing me back with the same vigor and desperation, and his hands slid onto my chest. He cupped and kneaded and massaged my breasts through my clothes. I wanted nothing more than for him to strip me naked and kiss me all over, for his mouth to find every intimate part of me and to push me over the edge until I couldn't take it anymore.

Bryce broke the kiss, and we were both breathing hard. His eyes were filled with lust that mirrored my own, but he swallowed hard and took a small step back.

A part of me sank in disappointment. He was putting a stop to this.

"You're tipsy," he said.

"So are you."

He nodded. "I know. But I don't want to do this when we're drunk. I want to do it when we're sober, and when we know what we want."

"I know what I want," I whispered.

Bryce smiled and brushed the back of his fingers down my cheeks.

"Me too." He kissed me on the tip of my nose. "But let's take it easy, okay? Let's watch a movie."

I nodded, swallowing my disappointment. He was being a gentleman, I reminded myself. I pushed aside the worries that he was no longer interested in me now that he'd had me once before.

He was being nice, and he still wanted to spend time with me. That was all.

He put on the giant flat screen television that covered nearly the whole wall it was mounted on, and I curled up on the couch next to him, buried in the crook of his arm. He closed his arm around me.

For a little while, I let myself believe that this was real, that this was how it was meant to be.

And that it wouldn't end.

CHAPTER 15

BRYCE

*T*his whole marriage thing for the sake of my job wasn't a joke. I'd thought it was a fucking good idea at the time—I'd given myself the proverbial pat on the back when I thought of it, and when Cora had unexpectedly agreed, I figured we had it in the bag.

What was six months' worth of pretend in the grand scheme of things?

Well, I was starting to realize the whole thing wasn't that easy. It wasn't just putting on a face and having another body around the house.

I couldn't return to business as usual.

I had to figure out how to make sure Cora's image was on point. And that was a hell of a lot harder than I'd expected. It wasn't that she wasn't the right person for the job—I was pretty sure she was exactly the person for the job. She was charming, intelligent, and beautiful. Plus, she was fun to be around. What was more, she was the girl next door.

Which was exactly what this company's image needed after I'd tanked it with my playboy ways.

Yeah, okay, so maybe I'd started seeing my dad's point

about my behavior. Damned if I was going to admit it to him, but I was starting to see the bigger picture.

And if I was being honest, I didn't miss my bachelor lifestyle a bit. The other women never even crossed my mind.

Still, Cora wasn't exactly what I needed her to be when it came to some of the board members. For some reason, even though Cora had nothing to do with the success of the company, Morrison and Stark expected her to be perfect.

So, in addition to running the company—which already a full-time job—I had to manage her image as well. Like I was suddenly dropped into public relations myself.

It was stressful as hell. I had sleepless nights and anxious days. But I would do whatever it took. The company was a gift to me more than it was a curse, and it was my father's labor of love. There was no fucking way I was going to let it all go to shit. I wanted to make something of myself, have a household name the way my dad used to when he was up here on the throne. Damn it, he'd spent more time here than he had with me when I was growing up. I deserved what was coming to me, at least.

But more importantly, I wanted to make my dad proud. I wanted him to know that I saw what he'd done and that I was taking my job seriously. I wanted him to know that I wouldn't let him down.

It was the morning of the gala. Cora and I sat at the kitchen table after a breakfast of fruit and omelets we'd cooked together. That was another thing I loved about her—she was a damned fine cook.

I had a folder in front of me and lifted the pictures of the board members one by one.

"Harry Sloane," she said.

I nodded and lifted the next.

"Carl Wentworth. Wait, that's Maxwell Parr."

"No, that's Charlie Brock."

She groaned, frustrated, and covered her face with her hands. "How am I supposed to get this all right? I haven't even spoken to half of them, and I'm supposed to know them just like that." She snapped her fingers for emphasis.

I nodded. "Look, I know it's hard. But you're doing great. So far, you've only gotten two wrong."

She looked like she was going to cry.

"Okay, okay," I said. "Let's change gears for a moment. What's the charity gala for?"

She blinked at me, her face a blank.

"Are you serious?" I asked, letting my own frustration creep in. "I thought it was straightforward."

"There's too much to remember," she said in a thin voice. "I'm sorry, okay?"

I let out a breath, trying to keep it together. Losing my shit at her wasn't going to help anyone, and it wasn't exactly her fault. I'd dropped her into the middle of all of this, and now it was like a crazy exam she had to pass.

"Save the…?" I prompted.

"Save the Shores!" she said. "They raise money to protect aquatic life from pollution."

"Right," I said, smiling. "Good job. Okay, who's this?" I lifted another photo, and her face sobered a little.

"John Morrison," she said. When I lifted another, "Louis Stark. Ugh, I'd never forget those two faces."

"You're doing great," I said, ignoring the discouragement in her voice.

She turned her head away. "Thanks," she said, but she didn't sound convinced. And that shot a pang through my chest. I was putting a hell of a lot of pressure on her to be perfect when I was pissed off that the board members wanted it in the first place.

I was technically no better than them, on some level.

"Let's take a break," I suggested.

Cora let out a sigh of relief and stood from the breakfast nook, walking to the coffee machine. She prepared herself a cup of coffee—her fourth in a row. This was really getting to her.

"Look, I know this is hard," I said. "And I can't tell you how grateful I am that you're helping me."

She nodded while she waited for her coffee.

"It's going to be okay. You're already doing so great, and tonight is about the bigger picture—it's not just Hollis Marketing employees and board members that will be there, but a lot of others, too."

She nodded again.

"Cora," I said and she finally looked up at me. "You're going to be just fine."

I hoped my words were reassuring enough for her. I didn't know how else to do it, how else to comfort her so that she would get through this okay.

Hell, how was *I* going to get through this?

I got up and left the kitchen, walking to my home office. I looked out of the window and tried not to freak out. The truth was I was losing my mind with anxiety over the gala. What if I'd made a terrible mistake going through with the fake marriage?

It was one thing if the whole plan worked, and we got out of this on the other end with me as the permanent CEO and Cora in the life she wanted. But what if the board ended up seeing through it? What if we were outed?

I hadn't given the downside to this whole sham a thought when I'd asked Cora to marry me. I hadn't considered what it might do to her if it came out that we were working together to cheat the system.

Not to mention what it would do to me if anyone found out. If news about this broke and the papers scooped it up, it was going to be a shit show and no matter how I tried to justify it, I would look like a terrible villain.

Sometimes, I wondered if I really was.

But when I was with Cora, everything felt different. I could almost imagine it going right, and the time we spent together always felt worth it.

What would it have been like if we'd naturally let our relationship develop after meeting by chance that day in the hall? How would things have been between us if we'd just dated and we could spend time together without all the added pressure?

But I probably wouldn't have given her much of a chance. Until recently, I'd been a heartless son of a bitch who'd taken what he wanted.

We would never have ended up together, and I would never have found out what an incredible person she was.

My mind drifted back to the gala. What if this whole thing failed completely? What if I was putting too much pressure on her, and she couldn't handle it?

My stomach twisted with nerves as I thought about what was happening and what the possibilities were. I had no idea if we were going to pull it off.

I needed this to succeed. Not only for my own sake, and my position at the company, but for Cora's sake, too.

I was determined to make it work, but there were so many variables, and in all my time working in the business world and learning how to take over from my dad, I had never felt so helpless and out of control.

CHAPTER 16

CORA

I dialed my mom's number and waited for her to find her phone and answer it. Sometimes, it took a little longer for her to get to her phone, so I held on until she had a chance to answer it.

"Sweetheart," she said, answering it just before it rolled over to voicemail. "Oh, it's so good to hear from you."

"Hi, Mom," I said, and tucked my feet under me on the bed. I'd come to the bedroom when Bryce had disappeared to his office. He was frustrated with me, I could tell. And that only made me more nervous.

"How are you?" I asked my mom. "How are you managing with Evaline?"

"She's a great caregiver, honey," my mom said. "She's not you, of course… I miss you."

"I miss you, too," I said.

Bryce had hired a caregiver to live with my mother as soon as I'd moved in with him so she would be taken care of. It was one of my conditions for the whole thing, and I was glad my mom was looked after. But I still worried. And I missed her a lot, too. It was strange not having someone to look after day in, day out. I hadn't realized how much time I'd taken out of my day to care for her, and even though it was nice to have some time to myself, I often didn't know what to do with myself.

Maybe it was because I wasn't in my own home, I was in someone else's space. Half the time when I was at the penthouse, I felt like I was intruding. It wasn't Bryce's fault, it was just bizarre—the whole thing we were doing was crazy.

"How are you doing?" Mom asked in return. "How's married life treating you?"

"It's real good," I said, forcing a smile so that it would sound genuine. I wasn't unhappy, but I was stressed and out of my depth. "Although, this is a new world for me. It's going to take some adjustment. To be honest, sometimes I feel left out."

I could be honest about that part.

"Honey, it's normal to feel that way. Marriage already takes such an adjustment and you moved very fast. It's going to take some time. I'm sure you're shell-shocked."

I nodded. That was exactly how I felt.

"I'm going to a charity gala with Bryce tonight," I said. "It's kind of fun dressing up—I've worn more ball gowns and cocktail dresses this week than in my whole life. But I'm nervous."

"What about?" Mom asked.

I took a deep breath. "That I'll mess up, somehow. I don't always feel like I belong. And I want to. This company is so important to Bryce."

"Honey, you'll be fine." Her voice was filled with confidence. She truly believed her own words. "You're resilient, you've always managed to do the impossible. And you have Bryce by your side. It's different now that you have someone who will be there for you."

It was like that, in a way. I supposed Bryce *was* there for

119

me. But it was for him, and if I made a mistake, he wouldn't be able to pick me up when I fell. I would drag him down with me.

"You need to talk to him about having some time away when you're able," my mom said. "I understand his work as the CEO is tough, but it's not right that you didn't get a honeymoon."

"We'll get away when we can," I said.

"You should have a honeymoon phase where you can be in love without all the distraction of the real world for at least a short while."

A pang shot through my chest when she said that. I still felt guilty that I was lying to her about it all. My mom had done everything for me. Keeping the truth from her felt so wrong. But she wouldn't understand what I was doing. I didn't want her to know that I'd been failing to make ends meet, and I didn't want her to know that this whole thing was nothing more than a business transaction. After how I'd been raised to believe that love wasn't the end game and that I didn't need a man, if she knew what this was really about, it would crush her.

She believed I'd found love, and after what she'd been through with my dad leaving her, I knew she was happy for me. I wanted her to be able to hold onto that happiness for as long as she could. I was going to rip it away in six months again as it was.

"I have to go," I said after we'd made small talk for a while longer. "I have to start getting ready."

"You're going to do great, honey," Mom said again. "You just need to believe in yourself. I love you, Cora."

"I love you too, Mom," I said, and we ended the call.

I dropped my phone into my lap and stared at it for a while. I missed being home. I missed my mother. And strange as it sounded, I missed my life. Even though it had been hard, even though there had been stress about money. It was a different kind of stress to what I had now.

I had never worried about who I was—I'd known exactly. Now, I felt like I couldn't be myself, and I wasn't sure who else to be.

I started getting ready. I put on the dress Bryce had loved so much and allowed a team of makeup artists and hair technicians to come in and help me get ready. It was important to Bryce, and I was getting to know my dress-up team better as we went along.

By the time we had to leave, I didn't recognize myself in the mirror, and I felt confident that I could figure this out. I felt almost invincible dressed up and made up like this, and that helped a lot.

After talking to my mom, I felt a little calmer, too.

When I stepped out of the room, Bryce was already wearing his tux. Had he dressed in another room?

He looked at me and his eyes slid slowly down my body and back up again.

"You look incredible," he said.

I blushed. "Thank you."

"I'm sorry about this morning."

I frowned. "What for?"

"I pushed you a little hard. I know you're doing your best, and you're doing a great job. I don't want you to think I don't have faith in you. I do."

I smiled at him. "I know you do. But I also know this is a big deal, and it's not easy on either of us. There's nothing to be sorry about."

He gave my hand a little squeeze. "I'm luckier than I realized."

Before I could ask what he meant, he turned and we left the penthouse together. We drove to the gala in silence. I could see Bryce's mind was far away, already on the job, and

I didn't want to distract him or interrupt his thought process. I'd seen that every time we were going to see important people, he shut down a little, retreating into himself. I didn't know if he was mentally preparing, but I respected the space he needed.

When the car pulled up in front of an ornate Art Deco building with red carpets leading up wide stairs, I leaned forward and glanced out of the window. Everywhere, men in suits walked around with decked out women on their arms. The couples looked important. And beautiful.

I swallowed. I looked just as good as they did, I knew that. I'd been made up to look the part. All I had to do was act the part, too.

Bryce climbed out of the car first and extended his hand to help me out. A few cameras flashed, the paparazzi getting their shots, as we walked into the building. I plastered a smile that I'd been practicing all week onto my face and walked with Bryce, head held high as if I had a right, just like everyone else, to be here.

Inside, there were no cameras allowed, and I could relax a little.

I looked around to see if I could spot anyone familiar when an unexpected face caught my eye.

Sal walked up to us.

"Dad," Bryce said, looking surprised. "I didn't know you'd be here."

"Wouldn't miss this event for the world," Sal said with a grin before he kissed me on the cheek. "You look spectacular, my dear."

I smiled at the compliment. "You look great yourself, Sal."

"If you don't mind, I need to speak to a few people," Bryce said.

"Go on, I'll keep her company," Sal said, and I was relieved not to be left alone again. The last time that happened,

Morrison and Stark had swooped in and I'd made a complete fool of myself. Plus, Bryce had told me that Sal knew about the sham marriage. And he didn't hate me for it. Knowing that made me relax around him.

"So, how are you handling the whole thing?" Sal asked after Bryce left. "Are you surviving?"

I nodded, glancing around. A waiter passed us with a tray of champagne and Sal grabbed us each a flute.

"It's a challenge, I won't lie. But I hope I'm getting it right."

"You certainly look like you are," Sal said. "And I'm sure there are a lot of jealous men here tonight."

I laughed. "You're being nice."

Sal nodded. "You deserve to know the truth. And I know it's not easy to do what you're doing. I don't think Bryce thought the whole thing through, but he's stubborn, and once he's set his mind on something... Well, that focus is a good trait in the business world, that's for sure. He's serious about making his mark."

"I noticed," I said. "But that's good. And I'm serious about helping him."

Sal nodded. "I can see that. And it means a lot to me that you've got his best interest at heart. This company... if he loses it, it will break him."

My stomach twisted. What if I were the reason he lost it? But no, I couldn't let myself think that way.

"He mentioned that it's just been the two of you and that the company is something you're both serious about."

Sal nodded. "Yeah, that's true. Bryce's mother walked out on us when he was very young. I doubt he remembers her now—which is a good thing. She was a piece of work, to be honest. My wife had a lot of issues, and she wouldn't have been good for Bryce, now that I look back at the whole thing. But the pain still lingers that his mother left him behind. I know it felt like rejection to him. When he was younger, he used to blame himself for it."

"I know what that's like," I said.

Growing up, I'd wondered if my father would have stayed with Mom if I hadn't been on the way. If she hadn't been pregnant, would he have held onto what they had?

Sal sipped his champagne and we watched more couples arrive.

"Now that I'm walking down memory lane, and you're kind enough to humor me, I'll tell you something else," Sal said. "I regret how much time I put into the company. That's for sure."

I wasn't sure why he was confessing such personal things to me, but I was willing to listen. I drank in everything Sal had to say about Bryce. I wanted to get to know him better. I wanted to understand him.

"I'm sure you did everything you could to give him the life he deserved, even when you were a single parent."

My mom had done that for me.

Sal nodded. "I guess I did. I certainly built the company with him in mind. But he couldn't stand competing with the company for my attention, and that drove us apart in many ways. I regret not being there for him all the time. And I worry that he got the wrong idea, that he learned the wrong lessons because of it."

I looked at Sal. This man who always came across as a giant in the media was just as fragile and emotional as the rest of us. He'd had his fair share of pain, too.

Knowing what Bryce and his father had been through only made me care more about them. They were both good men, even if they'd made some mistakes.

"I don't think you need to worry about it too much," I finally said. "Bryce knows what's important, and I think he understands what you did for him. I don't think he learned the wrong lessons."

"That's kind of you to say." Sal offered a weak smile.

I wished I could say more. I wished I could *do* more. I was in the middle of everything now, and I was getting invested in people I hadn't realized I would become close to. I cared for Bryce, and my heart went out to him and Sal and everything they'd been through—even more so because I'd been there, too.

I had to succeed at this. I wanted to make our marriage a success and convince the board that Bryce was a good CEO so he could build the legacy he wanted. I was determined to make sure he reached his goal of being the permanent CEO.

The rest of the evening was easier than I'd thought it would be. But we'd spent more time together lately, and he wasn't a stranger anymore. Every now and then throughout the evening, when we made eye contact, he smiled at me, and I got the idea he was happy.

Could I actually be doing it right this time?

CHAPTER 17

BRYCE

*T*onight, she made me proud. She'd done everything right. She'd gone above and beyond. I'd been nervous and anxious for nothing—she'd been spectacular from start to finish, and I was incredibly proud of her and how she'd transformed into exactly what I needed.

I felt a little guilty that I was expecting her to be something other than herself, but this was what she'd signed up for when we decided to get married, and I told myself I didn't have to worry about it.

Still, I did. But that was because I was starting to care about her.

Right now, I wanted to focus on the success of the night, our victory. I wanted to celebrate how well we'd done.

When we left the gala, it was after midnight, but I wasn't tired. Cora looked like she was on a high, too. Adrenaline pumped through my veins, and I was relieved and excited about how well it had gone.

"I was so happy to see your dad there," Cora said when the car pulled into the road. "It was such a pleasant surprise."

I nodded. "It really was. I didn't expect him there. But it was nice to have him around."

"He cares a great deal, you know," Cora said.

"Yeah, of course. If I go down, it will reflect badly on him, too. It isn't just my image we're trying to save."

"I meant he cares about you," Cora said. "About how you're coping with all this."

I glanced at her. I wanted to believe her—I'd wanted a close relationship with my dad for as long as I could remember. But I'd always known what was important to him: the business. Even though he'd done it for me, I wouldn't have minded if we weren't rich, if we didn't have everything. I would have been happy if we'd only had each other.

But the company was a big deal thanks to my dad and his hard work. As much as I would have preferred a relationship with him over it, the company was built now, and I was going to make sure that the one thing my dad and I shared, the one thing we had in common, would survive.

I appreciated that Cora had put it into words for me.

I was also glad she'd done so well. Tonight, the board had been impressed with her. They'd loved her. The way she'd acted had been perfect. She'd surprised me with her knowledge of my favorite foods and drinks, and she'd even made some references to a story from my childhood in front of a board member.

She'd really been paying attention the past week, and if I hadn't known that it was all a sham, I would have believed her act, too.

It had been amazing.

"Tonight was wonderful," Cora breathed with contentment.

"It really was," I said. "And I want to reward you for it."

She blinked at me. "What?"

"I want to give you something to say thank you. Anything, you name it and it's yours."

She looked a little confused. "You want to give me something?"

I nodded. Nothing I could give her would thank her enough for what she'd done for me so far, but I could try.

"What do you want?" I asked.

"You don't have to give me anything, Bryce," she said shyly.

"Come on, don't be modest. A tennis bracelet? A set of Tahitian black pearls?"

"No, I don't need fancy jewelry."

I'd never met a woman who wanted to be with me, and enjoyed what I was saying to her, without wanting what my money could buy. The women I had tried being serious with —years ago, before I'd decided to start sleeping around just for fun—had all wanted my money. The very mention of something expensive had made their eyes glitter.

But Cora wasn't like that. She was happy with nothing at all. Just sharing a laugh and a pretty sunset was enough for her. Sure, Cora's motivation for the marriage was the financial payoff. But I could tell she wasn't hyper-focused on wealth like most people I knew.

She was so different.

The car stopped in front of my building—our building—and we climbed out. Together, we rode the elevator to the top and walked into the penthouse. As soon as we were inside, I spun her around and kissed her. She yelped softly, but she melted against me the moment our lips locked, and I slid my tongue into her mouth, feeling her gasp lightly.

I leaned her against the wall right next to the door and pressed my body against hers, letting her feel my erection. I wanted her so badly. I couldn't explain what it was—it wasn't pure lust, a need for release that I felt with the other women I ran around with in the past. It was more than that. Deeper. I wanted to show her what I felt, because I didn't know how to put it to words. And I wanted her to know how much she was starting to mean to me.

She wrapped her arms around my neck, and I slid my hands down her sides, over the slippery material that clung to her body. Her curves were intoxicating, and as much as I loved that dress, I wanted her out of it.

I broke the kiss and took her hand, all but dragging her to the bedroom. As soon as we were in the room, I spun her around to face away from me. Slowly, sensually, I started unzipping her dress, letting it peel away from her body. I kissed her on the shoulder, feeling her smooth skin as it was revealed, and when the dress pooled around her ankles on the floor, she stood before me in only her G-string—the dress hadn't needed a bra.

I didn't turn her around again. Instead, I tilted her head to the side, my fingers lightly on her chin, and kissed her again. I reached around and cupped her breast with my free hand and ground my hard cock against her ass. She moaned and gasped as I touched her and kissed her.

I let go of her chin and reached down between her legs. I cupped her pussy, clad in lace, before I pushed my fingers under her panties and found her slit.

She was already wet for me, and I groaned.

"You're so fucking beautiful," I muttered against her neck.

I broke the kiss, let go of her, and turned her around again so that she faced me. I kissed her another time, cupping both her breasts, before I dropped to my knees. I glanced up at her, hooking my fingers into her panties, and slowly pulled them down. As I did, her scent wafted to me, and it made me dizzy with need for her.

I dipped my head and kissed her mound. She stepped out of her dress, taking a step back so that her back was against the wall, and she widened her stance, giving me space.

I pushed my fingers against her clit and drew small circles around it, listening to her whimpers and moans. The sounds she made when we were doing the dirty were so incredibly hot. It made me want to bend her over and fuck her right there.

But I was going to take my sweet time with her and taste every inch of her before I did anything else.

I wrapped one hand around her thigh and lifted her leg over my shoulder. When I leaned in and closed my mouth around her pussy, she cried out, and I stuck out my tongue, flicking it over her clit. I listened to the symphony of her cries and moans as I pushed her closer and closer to orgasm, my tongue flicking back and forth over her clit, sucking gently on her.

She was getting close, judging by her breathing, so I pushed two fingers into her entrance. She cried out when I did, and I started pumping them in and out, finger fucking her while I licked and sucked her clit. She pushed her hands into my hair, grabbing fistfuls of it, pulling me closer. She bucked her hips against my mouth, and I felt her fall apart, orgasming against my mouth.

"Oh, God," she cried out, breathing hard.

When her breathing evened out again, I glanced up at her and smiled.

"That was amazing," she said in a breathy voice.

I stood and kissed her, knowing she would taste me on her lips.

"You're still dressed," she said, and promptly started unbuttoning my shirt. She pushed it over my shoulders, along with my blazer, letting them fall to the floor.

When I was shirtless, she started kissing my chest, working her way over my pecs, my shoulders, my abs. When she moved back to my lips, her naked breasts pushed against my chest. Her nipples were hard, and there was nothing between us, nothing but my pants.

"Will you let me return the favor?" she asked, running her hand to my cock and cupping me through my pants.

I nodded and groaned. Never in hell would I say no to that.

I walked to the bed, unbuckled my belt, and pushed my pants over my hips.

Cora came to me and pulled my pants down further, and my cock sprang free, hard, and eager.

I lay back on the bed when she nudged my chest, and she clambered onto me. She straddled my legs and ran her fingers over my cock. I clenched my jaw as she lowered her head slowly, her hair brushing over my abs and my hips. Fuck, this was hot.

When she sucked the head of my cock into her mouth, I gasped, bucking my hips up. She sank her head lower and lower, taking an impressive amount of my cock into her mouth. She lifted her head again, swirling her tongue against my shaft as she retreated.

She started bobbing her head up and down, sucking me in and slipping me out, and the motion was a lot like sex, but totally different. She cupped my balls with one hand and massaged them while she sucked me, and I had to focus with everything I had to keep from releasing into her mouth. Although, God, that would have been incredible.

But I didn't want that. I wanted to finish inside of her.

"Babe," I gasped. "You're going to make me lose it."

She lifted her head, her eyes big, and fuck if I didn't think she was the hottest woman on Earth.

I pulled her closer to me until she leaned forward, and I kissed her. I slid my tongue into her mouth and kissed her like my life depended on it.

God, this woman was going to be the end of me if I wasn't careful.

I pulled her closer to me and kissed her again, running my hands over her body. Her skin was smooth and perfect, and her eyes were filled with affection and raw vulnerability.

Oh, God, I was in trouble.

Things were different with Cora, and it was becoming more and more clear. She was wonderful in so many ways, and nothing that I'd done before was the same with her.

If I wasn't careful, I was going to fall.

Hard.

But I wasn't going to think about that now. I was going to live in the moment and take what she had to offer. And I was going to give her what I had to offer in return. And this time, it had nothing to do with my pleasure and everything to do with hers.

I wanted her to know what she meant to me. And I was going to show her.

CHAPTER 18

CORA

*H*e was gentle with me, almost as if this was our first time all over again. But the way he touched me had a sense of urgency to it, a desperation that hadn't been there the first time.

And this time, my need for him echoed that urgency. Now that I knew what to expect and how it would be, I had a void inside of me that only Bryce could fill, an ache that I knew wouldn't go away until I got what I needed.

It was like Bryce was a drug I had lived happily without, but now that I'd had my fix, I couldn't get enough, I needed more.

I needed all of him.

I kissed him, pouring myself into that kiss, letting it all go. I had been reluctant to get attached, unsure about what it would mean to make a business deal that was so close to the heart.

Tonight, I didn't give a damn what could happen to my heart if I wasn't careful. All I cared about was getting as close as I could to Bryce and staying there for as long as possible.

"Hang on," he mumbled against my lips while he kissed me feverishly.

I pulled back, and he gulped as if he'd been drowning in me and had to come up for air.

I felt the same.

He ran his hands over my shoulders, his eyes sliding down my body and over my breasts like a physical touch before he rolled away from me and opened a nightstand drawer. He pulled out a condom.

I was glad he took the lead with that. I didn't think much about birth control. I was grateful he felt just as serious about it as I did, but it was hard to think about anything other than the raw need I always had for him. I didn't want to waste another moment when he could be inside of me.

Bryce opened the condom package and put it on in a fast motion, wasting no time. When he turned back to me, he kissed me again, tongue sliding into my mouth yet again, and I forgot all about it.

"You're so fucking beautiful," he muttered as he rolled me onto my back, pinning my body down with his weight. "Do you have any idea how incredible you are?"

I blushed wildly—I always blushed when he complimented me, even though it made me feel silly, like a schoolgirl. But the way he said it, it was impossible not to blush. He always made me feel like even though he'd said it to a thousand women, he hadn't ever meant it until now. With his tongue in my mouth, his lips locked against mine and the delicious weight of his body pressed along the length of mine, I couldn't answer.

If Bryce had expected me to say anything, he shouldn't have pushed himself between my legs. I opened my thighs for him, and the tip of his rubber-clad cock pressed against my entrance. I sucked in a sharp breath and felt him bore into me, only the tip. He stayed there for a moment, and I shivered and squirmed against him, needed him to go deeper, to slide all the way in and fill me up.

He didn't. He stayed right there, teasing me, causing the ache inside of me to grow until I roared with need for him.

"Please, Bryce," I moaned against his lips, the words coming out muffled.

He smiled against my mouth.

"I love it when you want me this badly."

"I do," I replied. "More than you can imagine. Please, just take me."

He hesitated, set on teasing me more, but finally his lust won out and he slid into me.

I cried out, letting out a breath of air as he drove into my core. When he paused, buried to the hilt, I shivered and wrapped my arms around his neck, my legs around his ass.

"I love being inside of you," Bryce said softly.

I kissed him. Telling him I loved it too, that it had easily become one of my favorite things, that this was all I could think about some nights, all sounded so cliché. I didn't know how to tell him what I felt when we came together like this, how I started losing parts of myself, and that having him inside of me completed me, putting me back together again so that I was whole.

He started moving, slowly sliding out of me until once again, only the tip was buried inside of me. I moaned when he slowly pushed his way back in again.

"You're set on teasing me tonight," I said.

Bryce chuckled devilishly. "I love working you into a frenzy before giving you what you want."

I moaned when he slid back into me again and squirmed on the bed as he repeated the process. Slowly—so slowly I barely noticed it—he started moving faster. After a while, he bucked his hips, pulling out and slamming back into me so fast, I couldn't keep up with my breathing. He forced the breath out of my lungs in rhythm with his fucking as he drew back and slammed into me again and again. As he moved inside of me, his body pressing down on mine, his cock pounding into me repeatedly, he pushed me closer and closer to an orgasm.

Bryce had a way of pushing me to the edge over and over. I hadn't talked to my girlfriends about sex all that much—I'd often felt shy about not having done it and didn't want to talk about it. But I was pretty sure multiple orgasms, like Bryce gave me, weren't as easily come by as he made it seem. He effortlessly took me from one plane of pleasure to another.

I couldn't think any more as my body started to contract, my muscles tightening and heat spreading through my body from my core, as if I was a cup being filled with hot water, and soon I was going to spill over.

And spill over I did. I cried out as pleasure washed over me, followed by a searing heat that was so incredible, I craved more of it whenever I wasn't with Bryce. I squeezed my eyes shut and let him take over, giving into the sensation of pure orgasmic bliss that filled my body.

When I finally came down from my sexual bliss, I blinked my eyes open to find Bryce staring at me with a lazy grin on his face.

"What?" I asked shyly.

"You're so hot when you do that," he said.

"What?"

"When you orgasm. And it's such a fucking turn-on to know that I'm the one that took you there."

I smiled, feeling the need to tuck my face away and hide my blush, but Bryce kissed me, and I wasn't going to turn away from that.

When he slipped out of me, I shuddered, missing him acutely.

"Turn around," he said softly.

I didn't waste time doing as he asked. I rolled onto my stomach and pushed up so that I stood on my hands and knees in front of him. I looked over my shoulder and wiggled my ass.

"God, woman," he said through gritted teeth, gripping my hips with both hands. "You're driving me crazy."

I giggled, but my giggle turned into a moan when he guided his cock to my entrance again and drove it into me. He slid in all the way so that his balls were pushed up against my pussy. I sighed, and he only gave me a moment to relish the fullness that came with him penetrating me before he pulled back and slammed into me again. I cried out as he picked up where he left off, not starting over or moving slowly but going ahead at full speed.

His balls slapped against my pussy, and the room filled with the sounds of our sex—our bodies coming together against the backdrop of our grunts and moans and cries.

I came again. I cried out and collapsed my chest to the mattress, grabbing onto the sheets and clenching them tightly. My ass was up in the air and Bryce rammed into me, fucking me hard as I cried out, giving over to the sensation completely.

After a while, Bryce pulled out of me, and I collapsed fully onto the bed. I knew what was coming—I'd started to get to know him, and I knew what he liked, how he wanted to finish. When he lay on his back, I clambered onto him, my legs like jelly. I sank onto his cock and moaned as he filled me yet again.

Every angle came with a new sensation, and I loved that he switched it up all the time.

As soon as he was inside of me, I started bucking my hips back and forth, sliding him in and out of me. This was how he liked it—this was how he wanted to finish. With me on top, riding him as if there was no tomorrow.

My breasts jiggled as I leaned forward and rocked harder and harder, bracing myself with one hand next to his head. The other hand was on his torso. I ran my fingers through his chest hair, relishing the feel of his skin, the sensation of his cock inside of me, and the friction of my clit on his pubic bone.

It didn't take long for me to work myself to the point of yet another orgasm.

I rode him harder and harder, crying out as I tried to stay on top of him and keeping my rhythm as long as I could, even though the orgasm was starting to render me useless.

I felt him grow inside of me. Bryce's brows were knit together, his face twisted in a mask of orgasmic pleasure, and I knew he was close.

Just a little more.

When the pleasure in my body rose to a peak, I cried out, and at the same time Bryce barked out a sharp cry. I felt him jerk and spasm inside of me as he came, and we came together.

I sank down onto his chest, riding out the ecstasy that crashed down on me like waves on the sand. Bryce's arms closed around my body, and I gasped as the intense pleasure took over. I let it wash everything away, leaving only the two of us in the midst of a sexual storm that seemed to last forever.

When we finally came down from the high we'd created together, I lay limp on Bryce's chest. His cock was still buried inside of me, but he was already softening. I could feel the change, with my body still clamped tightly around him. His heart beat against my cheek were I lay on his chest, and it didn't matter what the future held—right now, there was nowhere else I'd rather be.

I wanted this moment to last forever.

Eventually—I had no idea how much time had passed, but it felt like a long time—I rolled off him. He sat up and got rid of the condom without me seeing what he did with it. When he turned back to me, getting into the bed and holding the sheets open for me, I crawled under the covers too. I was slick with our combined sex, but the condom made it easier to go to bed without having to shower to clean up. It maintained the magic of the moment if we didn't have to break the spell.

Bryce pulled me tightly against him, and I loved the feeling of his naked skin against mine.

I lay on his chest, and his arm was curled around my shoulders. It was as if we'd been made for each other, and I couldn't believe I'd spent so much time telling myself I didn't need a man in my life when right now, I couldn't imagine anything else.

I started drifting off to sleep. Sometime, just before I dozed off, Bryce planted a kiss in my hair.

"You're becoming very important to me, Cora," he said.

I didn't know how to respond, and the way he'd said it made me feel like it wasn't wrong to say nothing at all. So I wriggled a little closer still, until the distance between us was non-existent, and I allowed myself to drift off to sleep.

When I woke up the next morning, it was as if neither of us had moved. We were still pressed against each other, clinging together as if we were each other's lifesavers.

I blinked up at Bryce, and he opened his eyes and grinned sleepily at me.

"Morning, beautiful," he said.

I smiled. "Good morning to you, too."

He kissed me, and I peeled myself away from him a little so that we could face each other, looking each other in the eye.

We lay in bed together, both of us in the main bedroom, and it was right. We belonged together. When we'd gotten married, when we'd started this whole thing, I would never have thought I would even think those words. But after how we came together, how our bodies merged until I had no idea where I ended and he began, everything was different.

Our physical relationship was incredible. On the one hand, I couldn't believe I'd waited this long to do it, to sleep with someone. I'd put so much weight behind it, feeling that it should be special, I'd missed out on something very intimate. But on the other hand, I was glad I'd waited this long. I was glad Bryce had been my first.

Somehow, I knew that it wouldn't have been this intimate if it had been with someone different.

Everything always worked out the way it should, one way or another. We didn't always understand why things happened the way they did, but it always worked out okay.

"What are you thinking about?" Bryce asked.

He lay on his side next to me, the sheets casually draped over his hips, barely hiding his sex. His naked body was becoming familiar to me. I was getting to know the shape of him, the lines and freckles and tiny scars.

"Actually, I was thinking I want to go back to work next week."

Bryce frowned. "Why? You have everything you need here."

I nodded. "I know." He was taking good care of me and my mom, making sure all our bills were covered, and giving me a home. It was very sweet of him. But it had all be a part of a deal that would eventually come to an end. And yes, at the end of it he was going to pay me three million dollars for it. It was so much money, I could barely wrap my mind around it.

But I wasn't going to be able to keep it all—most of it

would go to my mom's medical bills. And I still wanted to work. I wanted to get that permanent position. I wanted to make money of my own.

"I don't understand why you want to work," Bryce admitted.

"I like being independent," I said. "And I like working toward something. I'd like to work for that position and get it. I want to make my own money and make my own mark on the world."

Bryce nodded slowly, thinking about what I was saying.

"Okay," he said. "I guess that makes sense."

I smiled at him. I hadn't mentioned that I wanted to work because I couldn't put all my eggs in one basket.

Sure, I was Mrs. Hollis today. I was wearing his name right now, but it wouldn't last forever. I'd have to take care of myself again at some point. Even though I didn't exactly distrust Bryce, and it seemed like everything was going well with the board of directors, I didn't know for a fact that the money would end up in my bank account.

My experience with men was that good times never lasted. As charming and sweet as Bryce was, he was still a man. And men left you high and dry.

I needed to be able to pick up the pieces if something went wrong.

And I also wanted to be my own person. I had to earn my living, not because I was associated with Bryce, not because I carried around a name that got me things, but because I was good at what I did, and I deserved it.

After all, after six months, I was going to be just Cora Rhodes again, vaguely remembered as the woman who'd been married to the incredible Bryce Hollis for a short time.

My stomach twisted when I thought about it. And when I thought about leaving all this behind—leaving Bryce behind —my heart constricted a little.

What was this all about? How had it happened that I cared this much?

After showering and getting breakfast together, Bryce had to leave the house to take care of a few business things. Thankfully, I wasn't a part of them, and I could spend my day the way I wanted to. I felt like it had been months since I'd had some time to myself, although it had hardly been two weeks.

I picked up the phone and called Avery to arrange a coffee date. I missed my friend. I needed to catch up, to hang out, to do something normal for a change.

We met at Café Noir, a new place for me. When we sat down, I looked around.

"I love this place," I said. "Very modern."

The space had an industrial style, complete with raw concrete walls, exposed copper pipes and naked bulbs hanging from the ceiling. It was warmed up with deep red throw pillows on the booth couches, leafy green plants in copper pots, and jazz music that floated from speakers mounted against the walls.

"It's cool, right? I found it the other day when I came for a lunch break just to get out of the office. I swear, Dana is going to be the death of me."

"Is she driving you mad?" I asked.

"She's driving everyone mad."

I listened to Avery rant about everything Dana had been asking her to do, how unreasonable she was, and it made me miss the office life, being busy and working toward something. It only strengthened my resolve to get back into the office and keep working toward my goal.

"Well, on Monday I'll be there again to field the blows," I said. "Dana loves taking her mood out on those at the bottom of the food chain."

"You're coming back?" Avery asked, excited and confused.

I nodded. "Yeah, I can't just sit around and do nothing."

"No, I mean… are you still going to be an intern?"

"Sure," I said. "I mean, I need to do the work to get a permanent job."

Avery shrugged. "I guess so. I just thought Bryce would have given you a promotion or something."

I shook my head. "I don't need a promotion from him. Besides, I don't want to do it that way. I want the job because I earned it."

"That's very noble of you," Avery said. "I would have asked for a promotion, screw working my ass off to earn something." She grinned at me and I burst out laughing.

"I'm dying to know, how are things with Bryce?" Avery asked after our laughter subsided and our coffees arrived.

"They're pretty good," I said. "I thought it would be tougher than it is. You know… being *pretend married*." I whispered the last two words.

"He's easy to live with?"

"Yeah, he's not a total pig, and I have my own room."

Avery groaned. "You mean you're not sleeping with him yet?"

"Well, I didn't say that," I said, turning bright red.

"Oh my God, you *are* sleeping with him! Tell me every juicy tidbit! What does he look like naked? How big is everything?"

"Avery!" I laughed. "Let's just say that it's everything I dreamed of… and more." I hid my goofy smile behind my coffee cup as I took a sip.

"Cora, I'm so jealous of you right now! But you have to tell me more details. What's his apartment like? Do you have your own servants? A hot tub in your room? I'm going to need to see some pictures, too."

I laughed and answered her rapid-fire questions, leaving out any details that would have embarrassed Bryce. It was fun to talk to someone from outside my new world of luxury and comfort. It brought me back to Earth.

But there was a lot she still didn't know. Like how I was growing more attached to Bryce by the day.

Once she was satisfied with my answers, and I'd again made her swear not to breathe a word, Avery and I talked on. She complained about her love life—which was drying up right now, while mine was moving so fast.

It was good to get away from the fairy tale and the pressure I'd been under in the past weeks. Even though I strangely missed Bryce just being away from him for the afternoon.

When I arrived home, Bryce was still out. I had the penthouse to myself.

I walked through the empty apartment and looked around, trying to decide what to do while I had all this time to myself. I walked into Bryce's office and looked around. I ran my fingers over the heavy desk—he didn't have any family photos or personal items on it. He'd had his diplomas framed and hung on the wall, but there was very little about the office that reflected Bryce's personality.

Sal had told me that Bryce's mother left when Bryce was young. And I knew that Sal and Bryce had never been very close. It made sense that he didn't have anything familial on the walls or on his desk. I felt a pang of sadness that there was nothing sentimental in Bryce's life.

An idea started forming as I stood in his office, looking around at a place that was—albeit incredibly luxurious—very generic. I was only going to be in his life for six months, but we were still at the start of it, and for six months, we were going to have to give this a real shot.

I wanted to make the effort I would have made if we'd met by chance and taken the right steps to end up where we were now. And I wanted him to put a bit of effort into this, too. I wanted him to court me.

When he came home, it was almost dark and I was in the kitchen, cooking. I heard the front door and called out to him.

"What's this?" he asked when he walked in. "It smells great."

"I'm making Chicken Parmesan for us."

"It's a nice surprise," he said, leaning his hip against the breakfast counter. "I thought we would just go out for something to keep it simple."

I shook my head. "I wanted to have dinner in tonight. And talk."

"About what?"

I smiled at him. "I'll tell you over dinner."

He looked suspicious. "Come on, don't make me wait."

I chuckled to see the childlike, pleading look on his face. He really was a kid at heart. "Sorry, I'm not going to budge. Now, shoo. And change out of that suit."

When dinner was ready, I set the table for two and lit a couple of candles. I dished out two portions. Bryce came into the kitchen wearing jeans and a button-down shirt. I asked him to open us a bottle of wine, and he set out to do as I asked while I finished up the salad and carried the bowl to the table.

"Okay, what's going on?" he said when we were barely seated.

I laughed. "You can't contain your curiosity."

"I don't really like surprises. I'm not a spontaneous person."

I raised my eyebrows. "And yet you married me nearly on the spot."

"Touché." He cut into the chicken and took a bite. "Oh,

my God," he moaned, his eyes rolling back into his head. "This is delicious."

I smiled, thrilled that he liked it.

"Okay, so what's going on?" he asked again.

I looked at him, chewing my first bite and agreeing that it had come out amazing.

"I want us to date," I said.

Bryce frowned. "What?"

"You know, I want us to have a courtship. Go out on the town, write love letters, flirt… I want what normal couples do before they marry and move in together." I gestured around the room with my hand.

Bryce narrowed his eyes. "What for?"

"If we're going to pull this off, we're going to have to act like we really mean it. And what better way than to really woo each other?"

He seemed hesitant, unsure about what I was suggesting. I had the feeling that he hadn't really made this kind of effort with anyone—it wasn't necessary when it was just a one-night stand. But this was going to be a six-month thing, and we had to keep convincing everyone out there that this was as serious as we were saying.

"Okay," Bryce finally said, drawing the word out, still unsure about the whole thing.

But I smiled at him encouragingly. "Good. We'll start tomorrow. I think we should go to the beach together."

Bryce looked surprised. "The beach?"

I nodded. "We live in Southern California, Bryce. And the weather is great now. It would be a sin to ignore it."

He leaned back in his chair. "I don't know the last time I went to the beach."

"Then it's settled," I said and took another bite. "This is going to be fun."

He still didn't seem sure about it, but he nodded and continued eating.

I snuck glances at him as we ate.

If only I could know what he's thinking and how he feels about me.

I had a feeling he was just as confused as I was.

CHAPTER 19

BRYCE

Four months later

When Cora started her whole dating game—that's what I thought it was when she introduced it—I didn't think I was going to enjoy myself.

I didn't *date*.

I didn't make an effort. I didn't do personal or intimate or emotional. I'd always done physical and nothing more.

But as time passed, things started changing.

That first date on the beach had been a lot more fun than I'd expected. Innocent, wholesome fun. We splashed each other in the water. We laid in the sun until we'd nearly burnt to a crisp. I bought her an ice cream cone from one of the carts on the pier. Then I rolled in the sand laughing when she got chocolate ice cream all over her face just like a kid. She chased me into the water, and we made out in the waves.

It was perfect. And it was just the beginning.

As time when on, I started thinking of ways to make her feel special—I delivered a dozen red roses to her cubicle.

More than once. Sometimes, when I did, I snuck down to watch her turn beet red when she got the delivery.

We fell into a routine at home, too. What I hadn't expected was how we made time to spend with each other. And I loved it. I loved coming home early just to hang out with her. I loved being able to take her places she wouldn't have been able to go—movie premieres where we could dress up and walk the red carpet together, or elegant cocktail parties that weren't work-related.

There were plenty of work events, too, which I didn't love because I had to be switched on. But Cora was always on my arm, always dazzling, and she'd learned how to handle the board members, what to say and when to laugh, to stay in their good graces.

And they all liked her.

They liked her more than they liked me. At least, that was what it felt like some days.

"How are things going with Cora?" my dad asked one day when I sat in his office. We'd just wrapped up a business meeting at his place in Malibu—I'd driven there to spend the day before I headed back home for a date with Cora.

"Great," I said honestly. "A lot better than I expected it to go."

"I'm glad," he said. "I didn't think you were going to pull it off, if you want to know the honest truth."

I nodded. "I know. It was a long shot. There was one point when I wasn't sure, either. But it's been working out. I think it's because of this game she's playing."

My dad frowned. "What game?"

I sighed. "Well, it's not a game per se. But I'm calling it that to keep things in perspective. Because if I for just a moment allow myself to think…" I glanced at my dad.

"What?" he asked when I didn't finish my sentence.

"I know you don't really believe in love or anything, after what my mother did to you, but—"

"I never said I didn't believe in love," Dad said. "I do believe your mother was off her rocker, though."

I barked a laugh, surprised at his summary of the whole thing.

"If you find someone you really love, I'll be as happy as a father can be. That's all I want for you, Bryce. Happiness."

My heart squeezed a little when he said that. We didn't usually talk about mushy things like this. We usually kept it strictly business.

Lately that had changed, though. Maybe it was because we were more like equals now that I had taken over the company. Maybe it was because, aside from work, we were starting to have more in common. My dad liked Cora. She and I had been spending more time in Malibu with my dad.

Or maybe it was because Cora had told me after that first gala that my dad cared more than he let on. Maybe I'd started seeing everything he'd done differently.

Whatever it was, it made me feel I could try to talk to him about deeper things than the company.

"Well… I like her, Dad," I said. "Cora is amazing. In so many ways… I'm started to dread the six-month mark approaching, when all of this will be over."

He grinned at me.

"What?" I asked.

"I hoped something like this would happen."

I scowled at him. "Convenient for the business image?"

His smile faded a little. "No. Good for you. Cora is a decent girl, hardworking, serious about whatever she decides to put her energy into. And you change when you're around her. You become warmer, more approachable. But most of all, you seem happy for once."

I swallowed. I hadn't realized she'd done so much that I'd

changed. I knew everything else my dad said was true—she really was a decent person.

"So, you don't want this to end, huh?" Dad asked.

I shook my head. "No, I think I might want to do this for longer. I mean, this game..."

"Tell me about the game," my dad said.

I explained to him what Cora had suggested, how we'd started going on dates, courting each other, making a real effort.

"You can't call it a game," he finally said. "It's powerful. If more people did that in their marriages, the divorce rate would be lower. I think it was very smart of her to make sure it all worked out."

I nodded. "Yeah, it was smart. But I've fallen for her now. We're married, sure. But we're friends too. Thanks to all of this. I like being around her. I *love* being around her. And I don't know if she feels the same about me. There's a chance..." I hesitated, glancing at him before looking out over the incredible sea view he had from his patio. "There's a chance she's just going to take the money and run when all this is over. What do I do then?"

Dad frowned. "Have you asked her if she wants to stay?"

I shook my head. "That's not part of the deal."

He snorted. "Dating and courting weren't part of the deal, either."

"It's not that simple," I said.

I didn't know how to tell my father that I wasn't sure it would last because I wasn't used to women sticking around. It wasn't just about my mom, either. The women I'd been serious with before had all been there for my money. They would have stayed, but only so that they could keep tapping into my accounts. If I gave Cora money, there would be no reason for her to stick around. And since we'd agreed it would be over after six months, she had no reason to stay at all.

"I think you should talk to her," Dad said. "That's what couples do, right? Communicate."

"Right," I said.

"You've been doing everything else right. You should give it a shot. The only way you're going to get what you want is if you fight for it."

I nodded. I knew my dad was right. But the problem was I wasn't sure if it was what Cora wanted. I would fight for it, if I knew it was what she wanted, too.

But if she didn't want me, I would let her go. It had been our arrangement, after all.

Dad wanted me to talk to her, but I was worried about that. Not only because I didn't want to be the guy who told her I changed my mind about our deal, but because I was scared to find out if she was interested in more than just pretend, too.

Because what if she wasn't?

I acted big. I pretended like nothing could get to me, and most of the time, it worked. I could be invincible when I wanted to be. But Cora had gotten too close. She wriggled her way under my suit of armor.

And now I was vulnerable.

I didn't know if I could bear the rejection.

I left my dad's place, heading home to my wife, with mixed feelings. I knew I wanted more—more than six months, more than pretend. But I wanted to keep myself safe, too. I wanted to keep my heart behind high walls.

I had a feeling it was too late, though.

CHAPTER 20

CORA

I was late. Really late.

And I was barely holding back my panic.

"I've never been very regular," I said to Avery. "My periods have always been weird."

We stood in the convenience store in front of the home pregnancy tests. I wanted to walk away, to run and hide. I didn't want to be seen here. In my paranoia, it felt like everyone could see what I was doing here. But I couldn't run away from the fact that my period was late.

Not only a few weeks late the way it had often been before.

A few *months* late.

"But not *this* weird, right?" she asked.

I shook my head. "No, not this weird. I guess I've been in denial." I took a deep breath and let it out with a shudder.

"Come on, let's get one and get it over with," Avery said, reaching for a test on the shelf on my behalf because I seemed to be frozen. "There's only way to find out."

I nodded. She was right. I just didn't know if I could do

this. My stomach twisted when I thought about the possibility of being pregnant.

We'd been using protection, hadn't we? Bryce always reached for a condom. Always.

Except…

There was that one time we'd come home late from a gala. We'd gone at it on the couch, both of us so caught up in the moment we didn't stop to get a condom. So he'd pulled out instead.

Maybe that hadn't been the best idea.

It had only been one time. But then, it only took once, didn't it?

Avery walked with me to the counter, and I paid for the test. I used cash so that Bryce wouldn't know what I bought. Together, we went back to the apartment. Bryce was going to be at the office for some time—he usually tried to be home in time for supper so we could eat together, but tonight he was going to a board meeting that I didn't have to attend, so I would be home alone until late.

"Oh, my God," Avery said, looking around when she walked into the penthouse behind me. "This is where you live?"

She'd never been to the apartment before—I hadn't wanted to bring anyone here when it wasn't my permanent home. Soon, I would move back in with my mom, and this place would be nothing but a dream.

"Oh," I said, absently looking around and trying to look at it through the eyes of a stranger. "Yeah."

"This place is incredible! I wouldn't ever go outside if I lived here. How do you get to work every day?"

I laughed half-heartedly. "You get used to it after a while."

"I'm more than willing to conduct an experiment to see if I would get used to this."

We walked through the apartment to the main bedroom.

In the bathroom, I opened the pregnancy test. My stomach twisted and I felt like I was going to throw up.

Nerves, or morning sickness?

I hadn't felt any symptoms of pregnancy at all. Maybe it was just a scare. Maybe it was just a really delayed period and I was panicking for nothing.

"Two minutes," I said when I emerged from the bathroom again and looked at Avery. She lounged on the bed, running her hands over the thousand-thread-count covers.

"I know you're worried about this," she said.

"That's an understatement. I'm not ready for a baby yet. Especially when I'm not even in a real relationship."

"Try not to worry," Avery said. "No matter what, I'll be by your side. And maybe Bryce will be happy. Another little Hollis to take over the family business one day? Men eat that shit up when it's about legacies and stuff."

I nodded, not really knowing what to say. How would Bryce feel about that? And Sal? My father-in-law knew that this whole thing was a sham. What if he thought I'd intentionally gotten pregnant to trap Bryce, to steal their money?

I was getting ahead of myself. I had to find out what was real first. Maybe the test would be negative, and I'd been working myself up over nothing. Maybe it really was just stress—I'd been telling myself my late period was because I'd been under so much pressure, and even though Bryce and I were in a good space and I was a lot more comfortable around the board members, it was still a lot of work and responsibility.

When my two minutes were up—it felt like it had taken an eternity—I walked back into the bathroom and checked the test that I'd placed on the sink.

Positive.

Shit.

"And?" Avery asked from the bedroom.

I turned around and walked back to where she was sitting.

"I'm pregnant," I said, my voice almost a whisper. And tears promptly sprang into my eyes.

"Oh, Cora," Avery said, rubbing my back when I sat down. "This is major. But I know you're going to be fine. I'll support you, whatever happens."

She gave me a side hug, and I leaned into her, letting her try to comfort me. But there was no comfort to be had.

Pregnant.

Bryce and I were good together. We were really making this work, and I cared for him. A lot more than I should have, considering that this whole marriage was fake. But having a baby together? Our entire relationship was built on a false foundation, and to bring a baby into this world, when everything was a sham, a façade…

Thinking about it only made me cry harder, and the more I tried to swallow my tears, the worse it got.

Avery tried desperately to console me, but I was beyond help. I sobbed, breaking down from all the confusion and pressure I'd been feeling for months. I was grateful for my friend, but nothing she said made me feel better.

Eventually, she had to go.

"Call me when you need me, okay?" Avery said. "And good luck breaking the news to Bryce."

"Thank you," I said, my cheeks still wet with tears. "You're such a great friend."

"I wish I could do more."

I shook my head, assured her that she was doing everything right, and closed the door when she left. I leaned against it, new tears running down my cheeks, and I ran my hands over my lower stomach.

If this was from the time on the couch, the only time we hadn't used protection, I was almost three months pregnant.

Three months!

I'd picked up a bit of weight, but not so much that I'd thought anything was wrong. I'd figured it was because I'd been eating so many new and exotic foods living with Bryce. So I'd gotten a bit of a belly. Most women did. I'd started wearing looser dresses lately, so that it wasn't so prominent. And I'd tried to cut back on the carbs. Luckily, that meant I'd been staying away from alcohol, too.

But wasn't I supposed to have pregnancy symptoms? I hadn't felt any differently.

Except... I'd been going to bed earlier and earlier. Lately I'd been exhausted by 9 p.m.

And then there were all those days of upset stomach that I'd waved away as side effects of stress.

Now it all made sense. I felt like a fool. I guess I really *had* been in denial.

Avery had said I would feel better once I talked to Bryce about it. But what would I say to him? How would he take the news? Sure, he'd been putting a lot of effort into dates and spending time together, as I'd requested. But that didn't mean that he cared about me enough to want me around for the rest of his life. And it didn't mean that he wanted kids.

In fact, I was pretty sure he didn't want kids. He loved his carefree life. We hadn't ever talked about it outright—there had been no reason to. But he'd never mentioned children in any of his future plans. And when there were kids around us, he was blind to them.

All of this—our marriage for the sake of the company and the fun we were having away from it—was simply a temporary diversion. I was almost sure of it.

After our time was up, we wouldn't have to be married anymore, and he would move on.

What would happen to the baby then? The last thing I'd ever wanted was to be a single mother. I'd always vowed I would never let it happen to me, that I would never walk the same road my mom had been forced to walk. I'd seen how hard it had been on her, how much she'd sacrificed.

And now…

I started crying again, and I grabbed my handbag and headed out the door.

The only person that could make me feel better when it felt like the world was ending was my mom.

When I arrived at my childhood home, a wave of nostalgia washed over me. I'd been living with Bryce for almost five months now, and I missed being home. I'd come to visit my mom many times, but today it felt like I was here again for the first time since getting married.

Maybe it was my emotional state—it felt like my whole world was falling apart.

"Honey, what a surprise!" Mom said when I walked in.

She sat on the couch watching a television show like she always did in the afternoons. I studied her, and I was glad to see that she looked good. She'd been looking better every time I saw her lately, and it offered me a little peace of mind.

I sat down and hugged her. I buried my face against her shoulders, felt her arms close round me, and for a moment I pretended she could make all the bad stuff go away the way she always seemed to when I was a child.

"Are you okay?" Mom asked when I finally let go of her. She studied my face the same way I'd studied hers just a minute ago.

No. Everything is a mess.

"I'm fine," I said with a forced smile. "I just missed you."

She smiled. "I miss you all the time, honey. But I'm so glad you're out there, living your life. You deserve that."

"You know I didn't mind for one minute taking care of you."

My mom nodded. "I know. But it still wasn't right. You

should be in the world, doing your own thing. I should be able to look after myself."

I wanted to tell her that it was okay, that Bryce and I had this covered. But when I thought that, my stomach twisted and clenched. After this last month, Bryce wouldn't be there anymore. It would just be me again. And even though I would still take care of things, knowing I was going to have a baby to look after too...

"I have good news," my mom said.

I forced my own thoughts to take a backseat and looked intently at my mom.

"I went to the doctor yesterday, and he's given me the okay to start working again!"

"So soon?" I asked, worried.

My mom nodded. "My blood work is great. And I'm much stronger than I was before. Evaline and I have been going for walks. At first, I could hardly walk out the door. Now I can go for a half mile, and not even be tired afterward. It's good for me. I can't just sit here and do nothing anymore. I'm going to lose my mind. Now that I know I'm healthy enough to work again, I'm not going to keep sitting on my backside."

"As long as you're sure," I said.

"I am." She reached for a newspaper that lay on the coffee table. I noticed she'd circled a few different job listings, and while she told me about her plans, her eyes sparkled. Seeing her this happy made my heart swell. She'd been sick for so long, and knowing she was making progress made me relax.

I could finally believe that she would be okay.

"But enough about me," Mom said, putting the paper away after telling me everything, and settling back onto the couch. "How are you doing? How are you and Bryce?"

"We're doing okay," I said. "Better than okay, actually. But it scares me."

"Why?"

"I'm scared it won't last. What if all of this filters away and it wasn't real?" It sounded silly saying those words because I knew the whole thing was fake. But it was the marriage that was fake. What had been happening between me and Bryce the past couple of months felt very, very real.

"What do you mean?" my mom asked.

I shrugged. "I guess it all just feels too good to be true. I'm worried that one day I'll wake up and realize that everything he said he felt for me will turn out to be a lie. That he doesn't care that much at all and never did. What will I do then?"

My mom reached for me and took my hand. "I know you're worried because of what happened with your father. I always warned you to never to put all your self-worth in a man. But that doesn't mean that every man has bad intentions. And just because you're independent, it doesn't mean that you shouldn't invest in your marriage. I know this is scary—you haven't had any examples of what a relationship should be. But I have faith that you made the right choice."

I swallowed hard. I hated that I couldn't tell her the whole truth yet. Maybe, after it was all over and Bryce wasn't in the picture anymore, I would tell her what it was all about so that she wouldn't believe I'd been taken for a ride.

"I don't know what to expect for my future," I admitted. "I was so happy, but now I'm starting to wonder… what if it all changes? What if Bryce changes?"

"That's a risk we all take when we love, honey," Mom said. "I took that risk, too. Your dad broke my heart, but in the end, I got you. And you made my heart so full." She hugged me. "But the important thing is that I closed my eyes and jumped. I trusted. And you shouldn't mistrust Bryce because of our past, okay? He's a good man."

I nodded. I couldn't tell her about the baby, no matter

how much I wanted to. Not yet—I had to figure it out for myself first.

But was she right? Could I trust Bryce to be the man I thought he was? The man he'd showed me he could be? Or would he return to his playboy past?

Maybe the man I'd gotten to know was fake, along with the rest of our marriage.

I didn't want to believe that, but Bryce hadn't once mentioned anything about where we were headed and what would happen once our six months were up. I had every reason to believe that it would be the end.

I would have survived if things had simply ended. I could manage a broken heart, despite how much I loved him.

I gasped when that thought registered in my brain.

Yes, I loved Bryce.

But now that was I pregnant, everything had changed.

CHAPTER 21

BRYCE

*C*ora was acting weird.

What was really weird was that I noticed.

I'd never tried to understand women before. There was no point in doing that—they were in and out of my life in a matter of hours.

But with Cora, everything was different. I'd gotten to know her. I'd learned how to read her, how to hear the things she didn't say. I could pick up on the tone in her voice or see the look in her eyes. All that meant something.

And lately, she'd been distant and distracted.

She wouldn't tell me what was wrong, either. She swore she was fine, but I was starting to get the idea she was lying to me. She often looked worried. But when I asked her about it, she changed the subject.

I wasn't sure how to handle it.

"Ready?" I asked, walking into the main bedroom. I was dressed in a suit and tie, ready to head to the investors' meeting I'd been planning for weeks. I'd been in the office, working on my presentation for the evening, while Cora was getting ready.

When I walked into the room, she turned to me, head tilted as she fastened an earring to her earlobe.

She looked breathtaking in a wine-red dress, cut with an empire waistline, the high waistband decorated with crystals. It had little capped sleeves, and she wore jewelry to match the crystals on the dress. Her blonde hair was done up elegantly.

"You look great," I said.

"Thank you," she said, but she didn't smile the way she used to. She hadn't been responding to my compliments lately.

"Are you ready for tonight?" I asked. What I really wanted to say was, *Are you okay? What's bothering you? I can tell something's wrong.* But I knew she'd blow me off again.

Her responses worried me. Was she withdrawing because our marriage term was coming to an end? Was she detaching herself because she'd been waiting for this to be over and done with all along?

She walked to me, offering me a brilliant smile, but it didn't reach her eyes.

I returned the smile, searching her face, wishing she would talk to me.

We left the apartment, rode down to the lobby, and outside where the driver waited on the curb, I opened the car door for her. This was how we always did it—we'd fallen into a routine, a habit. I loved that we had created a life together, that we had made it work. I felt sick to my stomach when I thought about how all of this was going to come to an end.

I took a deep breath and shook off the feeling before I slid into the backseat next to her and shut the door so the driver could take us to the meeting at the office building.

We hosted a lot of the cocktail parties, meetings, and smaller events at the offices of Hollis Marketing. We'd set up the top floor the way it was for that purpose, paying a fortune in designers to make sure the space was right for that sort of thing.

When Cora and I walked in, most of the investors were already present. They stood around with drinks in hand, talking with each other.

Heads turned when we walked in. I knew it was because of Cora—she was stunning and everyone had come to love her. She'd really made an effort to win them over. So far, she'd held up her end of the deal perfectly.

Maybe that's all this was to her.

I'd thought she'd fallen for me, just as I had for her. Maybe it had all been for the sake of the deal.

I couldn't afford to focus on that right now. I needed to pay attention to the investors, to my presentation. The company was developing a new software product designed to revolutionize marketing campaigns. I was about to ask them to invest a lot of money in the company. I had to give them a good reason for it.

I cleared my throat, kissed Cora on the cheek, and walked to the front of the room.

The beginning of the presentation went better than expected—the investors were all interested, listening to my every word. As I talked, I glanced at Cora. She was looking out of the window rather than paying attention to me.

It frustrated me—what if the investors saw how disinterested she was and it affected their decision? Cora was supposed to be on my side, supporting me and making it seem like this was her whole life. Even if it wasn't. That had been part of the deal.

While I talked, I got more and more irritated. I hid it, masking it behind a smile. I finished my speech with dramatic flair, calling for a toast. Two waiters had moved through the group of investors, delivering flutes of champagne for all of them.

When one of them reached Cora, she refused the champagne glass.

I bristled a little before I lifted my glass in a toast.

All the investors joined in. It was a good sign. But I struggled to focus on the good when I was so frustrated with Cora and how uninvested she was in this, how detached she seemed from it all.

When the music started and the investors mingled, talking to each other, I walked to Cora. I shook a few hands on the way, engaged in small talk as I crossed the room.

When I finally reached her, she was standing to the side, alone, rather than talking to some of the investors.

"Can I talk to you for a minute?" I asked.

She nodded, and I walked to the door, stepping out into the hallway. Cora followed me and the music faded, the chatter staying in the room. We were wrapped in silence, and Cora blinked questioning eyes up at me.

"You've been very quiet tonight," I said. "Is everything okay?"

She nodded and smiled—one of those forced smiles that didn't reach her eyes. I'd been getting a lot of those lately.

"Everything's fine," she said.

"Are you sure?" I asked. "You know you can talk to me."

She nodded again. "I'm sure."

I bristled again, and the frustration surfaced. If she was going to be cold, well damn, I could be, too. Even if that made me a dick. But what was I supposed to do if she wouldn't open up to me? It took two people to pull off this marriage. I couldn't do it all by myself.

"I hate to have to remind you that we have a deal, Cora," I said coldly. "You promised you were going to fit in, to play the part." I smiled, trying to lighten the conversation a little—I realized I was getting too serious. Her eyes had dulled, and she looked unhappy with me. "I mean, this is all an act, right?

So, we should act the part. Both of us. You need to fit into the level of society I'm operating on."

I didn't know what I expected from her. For her to apologize? To buckle and tell me what was bugging her? To get emotional? I didn't expect an excuse or a fight, but instead of giving in the way I thought she would—the way she usually did—her expression turned steely.

"What's this all about, Bryce?" she asked.

"You're not mingling, for one," I pointed out.

"I didn't realize I was supposed to charm your investors in addition to the board of directors. I thought that was your job."

I blinked at her. She wasn't wrong, technically. The investors only had to like the company, not her. They weren't worried about the nature of our relationship—it had nothing to do with their money. But I wasn't going to let her win this argument.

"And you didn't join the toast," I added.

"Oh, the toast," she said.

"You can't tell me you didn't think it was important to toast the new direction we're taking," I said.

She tilted her head to the side a little. "No, you're right." She folded her arms over her chest, but it didn't seem defensive. Instead, it seemed almost confident. "Well, the reason I didn't drink champagne was because I'm pregnant and there's no fruit juice to be had. I checked."

I blinked at her. "What?"

"Your waiters didn't bring anything non-alcoholic."

I shook my head. "No, the other thing." My voice had gone strangely breathy.

She looked at me, her face serious, and I knew she was telling me the truth. She wasn't fucking with me the way a tiny part of me hoped she was. I was already starting to feel lightheaded, my ears ringing. I fought hard not to sway on my feet.

I heard what she'd said. But I needed her to say it again.

"I'm pregnant, Bryce."

CHAPTER 22

CORA

I didn't expect Bryce to react to the news very well.

I'd been wrestling with how to tell him. I hadn't meant to drop it on him like a bomb at one of his most important meetings, but the way he'd challenged me and suggested I hadn't done my bit had just pissed me off.

I had sacrificed my life for him for the past five months. Sure, it was for money, I wasn't going to walk away from this thing empty handed. But the way he'd reminded me of my promise, as if I was someone he needed to scold, someone who let him down, just made me snap.

So, I told him.

After I told him I was pregnant—twice—I watched as all kinds of emotions played over his features. He went from shock to confusion to anger. His eyes grew stormy, and he clenched his jaw.

He looked like he was about to lose it. But there were investors right on the other side of the wall, and they would hear our fight if it went that far.

There was no way Bryce would allow that to happen. His

investors were vital to the next step for the company. And the company, to Bryce, was everything.

So, instead of losing his mind and saying all kinds of nasty things to me—I was sure he could have come up with many—he cleared his throat.

"We'll have to talk about this later," he said. His teeth were gritted together and his eyes were so cold, I shivered just looking into them.

"I guess we will," I said, my tone even, although my bravado from a moment ago was starting to slip.

It had been easy enough to be swept up in the moment, to come out with it as if I wasn't shattering both our worlds with that information. But now I was starting to come down from the adrenaline high that had allowed me to do that, and I felt small and fragile. I just wanted to turn around and run away. I wanted to find a dark, empty little corner and hide away from the world.

But there was no getting away from this—not from the pregnancy or from the snowball I'd just set in motion by breaking the news to Bryce so bluntly.

Besides, he'd accused me of not keeping up my end of the deal, and there was no way in hell I was going to turn around and walk away now, proving him right.

He pulled himself together, plastered a smile on his face, and stepped back into the room as if nothing had happened. I followed, forcing a smile of my own, hoping it looked genuine enough. Bryce had years of practice wearing a poker face. Mine wasn't nearly as well-rehearsed.

But somehow, we managed to pull it off. Despite the tension and the vibes between me and Bryce, the investors seemed happy. We had to make small talk and schmooze, charming the people who were going to throw loads of money at Hollis Marketing. But whenever Bryce touched me, it lacked the warmth his touches usually had, and when he looked at me and smiled, it was so brittle, I was sure his friendly expression would crack and break at any moment.

It felt like forever before we could go home. By the time we left the office—the last to leave after the meeting—my feet were sore from the heels, and my lower back ached. A symptom of pregnancy, I'd found when I'd looked up what I could expect.

We rode the elevator down to the lobby in silence. The tension grew thicker and thicker, but Bryce said nothing and I had no idea how to start. What was I going to say to him? What was there to say to each other at all?

There was a lot to talk about, but not like this—he was furious with me. And I wasn't in the best head space, either.

When we sat in the car, the partition between us and the driver raised so that we had our privacy, Bryce exploded.

"Who the hell do you think you are?" he challenged.

"Excuse me?" I asked.

"Do you think this whole thing is some kind of sick game? Did you think if you played your cards right, you could get what you wanted?"

I blinked at him. "I have no idea what you're talking about."

"The pregnancy!" Bryce cried out. "I know what you're doing, Cora. I see right through you. Don't you dare think I'm not onto you. I've known plenty of women like you in my life, so don't think for a second I'm stupid enough to fall for you tricks."

He all but spat the words at me.

"What is it that you think I'm doing?" I asked. My mouth dropped. He seemed to think I had some kind of agenda. He was angry about... something. But not about how he'd found out about the baby, which was what I'd thought would be the biggest issue.

"If you think this ploy will keep you around, if you think

I'm going to let you dig your fingers into my wealth just because you're carrying my child, you've got another thing coming."

I gasped. "What?"

"You're just like everyone else," he said, waving his hand at me. "You're a gold digger like the rest of them. Well, I've got news for you. I'm not going to let you play me like this, having the baby just so you can leech off me."

"What the fuck is your problem?" I cried out, cutting him off before he could keep saying things that hurt like hell. "You think I planned this?"

"What else?" Bryce asked, seething. "It's damn convenient for you to get pregnant so close to our deadline, isn't it?"

I couldn't believe what he was saying. A ploy? I played him to get his money? His words shocked me to the core. They hit me like physical punches, and I struggled to wrap my mind around his thought process.

"Do you think I got pregnant on my own? You do know where babies come from, right?"

"We were careful," he shot back.

"Not always. Obviously. And no, I didn't poke holes in the condoms, if that's what you're thinking."

He crossed his arms over his chest and looked out the window.

"How long have we been married?" I asked.

"Five months," he said, sounding frustrated that I was asking him obvious questions.

"And in that time," I said, "didn't you get to know me somewhat?"

"I don't know you at all," Bryce sneered. "How could I? It's not like this marriage is real."

I'd been trying to keep my cool, but that was the last straw. I snapped.

"You're right," I said. "It's all fake. Every single part of it.

How we acted toward each other, how we cared for each other, the time we put into dates and spending time together even when the rest of the world wasn't looking. It was all an act, wasn't it?"

He was quiet. I studied his face, searching for some sign of the truth. Had it just been an act to him?

If this was his response to the pregnancy, he must have been acting the whole time. How else could he accuse me of trying to steal his money?

The realization pierced me like a knife in the heart.

He'd never cared for me.

The car finally stopped in front of our building—his building—and I jumped out of the car and hurried inside before Bryce could say anything else. My face grew warm as tears filled my eyes. I stumbled, struggling to move fast in my high heels. I pressed the button for the elevator repeatedly, afraid he'd catch up with me before I could get away. The last thing I wanted was to be caught in another small space together.

The elevator doors slid open, and I stepped in, pushing the button before Bryce walked into the building When the doors slid shut, I let out a breath I didn't know I'd been holding.

But it was far from a breath of relief. Tears ran over my cheeks. A strange emptiness filled my chest.

Upstairs, I opened the apartment door, closed it behind me, and leaned against it for all of two seconds, trying to pull myself together.

What was going to happen now? I had no idea. How could I keep doing this, even if it was only four more weeks, now that I knew Bryce thought the worst of me? What would it do for the company and Bryce's image if I left now?

A part of me wanted to throw caution to the wind and

leave. I shouldn't care what happened to Bryce and his company if I pulled out early.

But I couldn't do that to him. I'd made a promise, and I wasn't someone to just go back on her word. Besides, I needed the money. If I got out now, the verbal contract between us would be null and void and I wouldn't get anything. I still had bills I needed to pay, and even if my mother was doing better and would be working again soon, it wasn't enough. Whatever job she found wouldn't cover the mountains of medical and credit card debt.

But aside from the money and the fight and the words that hurt terribly—I couldn't leave Bryce. I still cared about him.

I shouldn't have fallen for him, but I had. And I wanted to make sure our plan was successful. Even if it meant that we would walk out of each other's lives after this and I would never see him again.

Just as my own father had abandoned my mother and me.

The very idea shot a terrible ache through my chest.

CHAPTER 23

BRYCE

*T*here was no way in hell this was going to end here. She wasn't going to get away with this. I couldn't believe it—we'd been doing so well! And now, just as we were in the home stretch, she threw a wrench into the whole thing. If we weren't careful, all our hard work would go down the drain.

She thought it would be as simple as getting out of the car and running inside. Well, she had another thing coming. She wasn't going to get off this easy. The term wasn't over yet—we still had another month before the deal was up, and no matter how fucked up this whole thing had just gotten, she wasn't going to ruin it all. We were so damn close.

I let her get ahead for a moment, taking the time alone to pull myself together. I was so fucking furious I couldn't think straight. Adrenaline pumped through my veins, and my head spun a mile a minute, going over all the facts.

The only thing I knew was that Cora had fooled me. I'd thought she was different.

I was wrong.

The hate in her eyes had revealed the truth. She'd never really cared for me. She'd been acting this whole time.

And now she was pregnant. Whether it was accidental or not, she'd hidden the pregnancy from me for two weeks. That was how long she'd acted weird and secretive around me.

She'd pulled away from me and insisted nothing was wrong. Why hadn't she just told me the truth right away? It would have been a shock, but we would have figured it out.

But the secrecy, the distance—maybe she'd been biding her time. She'd been planning her next move, calculating how best to use the pregnancy against me.

Or maybe she'd intended to keep it a secret for another month, until the term was up. Then, she could quietly leave and raise her kid—my kid—alone.

Either way, I meant nothing to Cora.

Because if I did, she would have told me right away. She would have included me.

I'd felt so close to her. I'd thought she felt it, too—this special connection between us. But if she had, she would have leaned into me.

The intimacy I thought we shared was just an illusion.

I wasn't sure how to feel about the fact that she was pregnant. I knew that I was going to be there for the child, but not in the way Cora no doubt wanted this to pan out. No doubt she wanted me to never even meet the kid.

I wasn't going to let that baby grow up in a home where they felt they weren't wanted. I'd grown up that way, and I wouldn't wish it on anyone.

I climbed out of the car and marched inside, hearing the driver pull off. I could only hope the partition separating us had kept him from hearing our fight. Otherwise, it would find its way to the tabloids.

Lucky for me, and unlucky for Cora. With the media on

her side, she might get what she wanted. But right now, I had a leg up. We could figure this out in private. I just needed to tell her how things were going to be.

We needed each other. That was what all this was about—I needed her image, the façade of a marriage so that I could keep my position in the company. And she needed my money. I would prove that to her, but she had to understand damn well that it wasn't going to change now that she was pregnant. I wasn't going to let her take me for a ride on her terms.

The apartment was lit but quiet. I searched for her, storming through the rooms. I found her lying in bed, still in her dress.

"I can't do this tonight, Bryce," she said, sounding defeated.

It tugged at me for all of a moment before I shook my head. I wasn't going to let her get away with this. It had been a game this whole time, hadn't it? And I'd fallen for it for far too long.

"Well, that's too bad," I snapped. "Because we're doing this tonight."

She looked weary when she glanced up at me from the bed. Seeing her like that, raw and vulnerable on the sheets, my dick punched up in my pants.

Damn it, what was wrong with me? But she was so fucking hot, and no matter how hurt I was by this whole thing, something about her would always be attractive to me.

"I know what you're doing—" I started, but she cut me off.

"You have no idea what I'm doing! You think this is all about your money, but I don't give a shit about your money!"

"Yeah? Then why did you marry me in the first place, if not for the money?"

She rolled her eyes. "That was because you practically

blackmailed me into marrying you, and we had a deal. That's not the same as this."

"How's it any different?" I challenged. I wanted her to say it. I wanted her to tell me it was about my money, so that I could hear it from her mouth.

"I'm not after your money, Bryce. Didn't you learn anything about me and who I am over the past five months?"

I didn't know what to think anymore. If I had to go by what we'd become to each other—what I'd *thought* we'd become—it would have been a different story.

But maybe Cora's care and affection had been one big lie.

Hell, we'd both been acting all this time for a bunch of different people. Maybe this was just one more illusion from her.

The biggest illusion of all—making me think she cared for me.

Her eyes narrowed when I didn't answer her.

"You think I'm lying to you," she said. A statement, not a question.

Again, I didn't answer.

"Fine," she finally said. "You think money is what it's all about? Then keep it. I don't want any of it."

"What?" She caught me off guard with that.

"The three million. I don't want it. You think I'm just after your money? Well, you can relax now. I won't touch a cent of it."

I blinked at her. This didn't make sense. Now she was pushing it all away?

And throwing me away in the process.

That yanked me back to a time when I wasn't wanted, when I wasn't good enough. My mom had left without taking me with her. And now, Cora was doing the same. She was going to leave.

Man the fuck up, I told myself. *You don't need her.*

177

But I couldn't help myself. I couldn't help but feel that she'd used me all this time. And I hated it because she'd fooled me. I'd believed she was genuine.

Damn it, I was such a fool!

"Fine," I said tightly. "But you're making a mistake."

She gasped. "Make up your mind! First you accuse me of wanting your money and then when I don't want it, I'm wrong?"

"This isn't about my money anymore," I sneered. "This is about me. You were never serious about me, were you? You never wanted me."

Cora groaned. "We didn't get married because of our feelings for each other, Bryce."

Her words sliced through me like hot knives.

Even though she was right. This marriage hadn't been about love. Hell, I'd used her just as much as I was accusing her of using me. But over the past few months, things had changed...

At least, they'd changed for me.

"You won't find someone like me again," I said, walking closer to the bed. "Not another husband, not if you're acting like this. And not another chance at millions, either."

She looked at me, her eyes filled with something I couldn't read. A ton of emotion, but something so fucking sexy, too, I struggled to think straight.

"I'm done with this conversation," she said, getting off the bed on the other side from where I was standing, and walking away from me.

"Where are you going?" I asked.

"Away from here," she said. "You're being cruel. I get it, you're hurt. You think I planned this, but it was as much of a shock to me as it was to you, Bryce. And after all this is over, you'll come out on top. You'll be the CEO of your precious company. But me? I'll go back to my old life, without anything to show for the months of effort I put into this. Nothing except single motherhood."

She walked out of the room, and I stayed behind in the wake of her words.

But no, she wasn't getting away with it that easily.

"Don't you dare," I said, following her through the apartment and into the kitchen. "You think I'll just keep going without a hitch after this?"

She whirled around. "Of course! You're still getting what you want, Bryce. And that's what it's all about." She laughed sarcastically. "You keep pointing a finger at me, saying that I used you, but what do you think you did to me?"

We stood close to each other, and the anger crackled around us like static in the air. But I was suddenly aware of how close her body was to mine, and I couldn't help myself. My world was crumbling, but somehow the sexual tension in the air was so thick, it replaced the anger.

Could she feel it, too? Or was I the only one that thought about fucking in a time like this? God, I was a fucking mess if I thought...

Her eyes slid to my lips, and she leaned slightly toward me. She felt it too—there was no way she'd missed it. There was no way...

When her breath hitched in her throat and her eyes slid up to mine, filled with hunger and need rather than anger, I was done holding back.

I grabbed her and kissed her. Hard.

For a moment, she froze. I waited for her to react—either to kiss me back or to pull back and slap the living shit out of me before storming off. It felt like a lifetime passed between the moment I grabbed her and the moment she responded. Instead of slapping me, she melted against me, and opened her mouth so I could slide my tongue inside.

Our anger and frustration translated into pure, unadulterated need for each other, and I started peeling her clothes off her body. With one hand I cupped her breast, and with the other I reached around her and unzipped the silky-smooth material of her dress. When I pushed the straps over her shoulders, the material fell to the ground in a swoosh and pooled around her ankles.

She stood before me, dressed only in heels and underwear, and she was incredibly beautiful. Her eyes were filled with hunger, and I grabbed her and kissed her again.

Her fingers fumbled with at least half my buttons before they moved down to my pants. I took care of the rest of the shirt, pulling it off me while she got my cock out of my pants.

She started sinking to her knees, but as much as I loved it when she sucked me off, I wanted to get inside of her. I had a raw, animalistic need to take her and make her mine.

"Don't," I said, pulling her into a kiss again. I lifted her up, hands under her ass, and placed her on the kitchen counter. She gasped when the cold marble pressed against her skin, but her breathing was erratic and she kissed me back, matching my feverishness with her own.

I tugged at her panties and she lifted herself enough for me to get rid of them before I pushed her backward on the counter. Thank *fuck* I'd cleared it off earlier today.

I kicked off my pants, yanked my boxers down as far as I could while I climbed onto the counter, and her legs fell open for me.

It didn't take me long to find her entrance, and she was dripping wet for me. I groaned when I pushed into her, my cock finding her like it had a homing device on it, and she moaned long and loud as I slid into her.

I started bucking my hips, not wasting another minute.

Her eyes locked on mine as I fucked her, her body

rocking back and forth on the cold marble, her breasts still tucked into her bra.

I grabbed her left breast, pulling down the cup, and dipped my head. I sucked on her nipple while I slowly slid in and out of her, and she gasped and moaned. Her hands were on my shoulders, holding on for dear life.

I was getting close. I wanted to release inside of her. I wasn't wearing a condom, but I realized with a sudden pang that it wasn't necessary. She was pregnant.

The thought scared me. I pushed it away and focused on the here and now—on the way her body clamped around my dick, the way she wrapped her legs around my ass to pull me in deeper, and the way she gasped and moaned, large eyes boring into my soul, lips parted. She was so fucking sexy, I had no idea how I was going to live without her.

I pushed that thought away, too, and started fucking her as if there was no tomorrow. Because hell, who knew what would happen after tonight? All I knew was that right now, she was here with me. I was buried inside of her, and this was where everything felt perfect between us. We were one, and our life together was incredible.

That was all I was going to think about. That was all that mattered.

Not the pregnancy, the money, the agreement... nothing mattered more than me and her, right here, right now.

She orgasmed wildly, her nails digging into my skin with little warning, and the way she cried out and thrashed beneath me only pushed me over the edge, too. The sharp pain on my shoulders intensified the orgasm, and she climaxed while I released inside of her.

The sex was fantastic, more intense than anything we'd had before.

When I jerked one last time, emptying myself completely, Cora turned her head away, not looking at me.

I pulled out of her, breathing hard, before I hopped off the counter and found a box of tissues. I handed it to her and turned my back to give her a bit of privacy, pulling up my boxers while I waited for her to clean up.

When she was done, she cleared her throat. I looked up at her, and the sexy vulnerability was gone. She had closed off from me, and I felt an acute absence.

"I'm going to shower and get ready for bed," she said softly.

"Okay," I answered.

She left the kitchen, carrying her clothes draped over an arm. I watched her in a daze.

Fuck, everything about Cora was a dream. But it wasn't real—none of it had been.

And it was time to wake up.

CHAPTER 24

CORA

When I opened my eyes, I felt sick.

My stomach turned and my head ached dully. When I opened my eyes a crack, the world spun around me. It was a hangover minus the alcohol.

The room was brightly lit. The curtains were open, and the light had woken me.

When I turned my head to the side, the bed was empty— Bryce wasn't here next to me. I ran my hand over the mattress. It was cold, the bed made on that side. He hadn't slept in the same room. I knew I had pulled back emotionally after our intense sex last night. But a part of me had hoped he would have slept next to me.

It was silly.

More details of the previous night came back to me like a flood, and my eyes stung with tears. God, he'd been so mad. So intense, so accusing. And at the same time, he'd been so incredibly hot. Our sex had been amazing—the best sex we'd ever had.

But what did it mean? Had it been Bryce's way of getting rid of excess emotions, trying to reach me despite what had happened between us? Or had it been a way to say goodbye, to end things?

I had no idea.

My stomach turned again. I jumped up, running to the bathroom. I threw up into the toilet bowl, retching and heaving, but producing very little. I hadn't eaten yet, and my stomach was empty.

It was ridiculous—now that I knew I was pregnant, suddenly the morning sickness happened all the time. Almost as if the little life growing inside of me had waited for me to figure things out before making itself known in full force.

After throwing up, I sat back on my heels and wiped my mouth with a tissue. I stood, washed my hands and brushed my teeth, and walked back to bed, sliding in between the covers. I didn't want to get out of bed, get dressed and go into work. I didn't want to do anything at all. I wanted to lie here in bed and stew over what had happened last night.

I wanted to feel sorry for myself. I needed time to wrap my mind around what was happening now.

The fact was that I was having this baby. No matter what happened, no matter how Bryce acted—whether he was a son of a bitch about it, or kind and welcoming—it wouldn't change things. I was going to be a mother.

Last night, he had been furious, accusing me of all kinds of terrible things. But the way he'd looked at me, the way he'd touched me, had been so filled with other emotions, I didn't know what to think.

Bryce knocked on the door and pushed it open, bringing a tray of food.

I frowned.

"Hi," he said carefully.

"Morning," I answered.

He walked to me and put the tray on my lap. He'd made

scrambled eggs with hash browns and coffee. The smell rose to my nose, but instead of stirring my appetite, it only made me feel sick again.

"So, about last night..." Bryce started.

Was this an apology of sorts? Why was I getting breakfast in bed?

"Yeah?" I asked, not willing to put any words in his mouth.

"Well, I've been thinking. I know you said you don't want my money. And I may have gone too far by accusing you of scheming to take it..."

May have gone too far? I raised my eyebrows.

"The thing is, it's my child you're carrying. And I'm not going to let you walk out of here to fend for yourself alone. So, I'd like to give you some money after all of this, for whatever route you want to take, even if you leave before the six months is up."

I blinked at him, waiting for him to say something else. When he didn't, my stomach sank.

Whatever route I wanted to take. In other words, he wasn't going to be there.

I looked at the food, and instead of feeling grateful that he was trying or happy that he had come to his senses when it came to caring for the baby, I felt sicker than before. My stomach turned again, but this wasn't just morning sickness.

He'd rejected me again.

"I can't believe you're doing this," I said softly, starting into the coffee on the tray.

"What?" Bryce asked, clearly confused. "I thought—"

"That everything would be fine if you threw money at the problem?" I snapped, interrupting him. "I know that's usually how it works in your life, but that's not how it works with children. Children need more than that. They need involvement. You of all people should know that."

His face blanched. I knew it hadn't been the right thing to say. But damn him, I was furious that he was trying to smooth it over this way. Did he really think breakfast in bed and money would fix everything?

"I'm trying to do the right thing, Cora," Bryce said. His voice was calm, but his eyes were dark. He clenched his jaw, biting back his anger.

What did he have to be so angry about? He wasn't the one whose entire life was about to change. He didn't want to be here for us. And I realized I wanted that more than anything —I wanted Bryce to be here for me and the baby. I wanted this life we'd created together to have a chance, to work out.

But Bryce was hardly father material—God, five months ago, he'd been a serial womanizer. The only reason his behavior had changed was because he'd been about to lose the company.

He didn't stop chasing models because he wanted to be different.

Now, by offering me nothing more than cash, he was proving to me that he wasn't the right person to be a father to this baby. He didn't want to stick around. He was going to leave—a second baby born without a father. Just like I had been.

My heart twisted, and I switched off, pushing my emotions away as far as I could. Damned if I was going to cry in front of him, let him know how upset I was.

"You never meant to be around after this, did you?" I asked.

"Why would I? It wasn't part of the deal." His words were tight. He turned away.

That hurt. "And now that there's a baby?" I asked.

He hesitated. "Look, I said I would give you money so you could take care of yourself. Without a court order, without getting any asshole lawyers involved. I'm doing the right thing, Cora."

"The right thing?" I asked, my voice raising. "You're just like the rest of them! All men are the same. You stick around for as long as it's convenient. The moment a shiny new object enters your vision, or things get a little too heavy, you leave."

"Don't you dare," Bryce said softly. His quiet anger was almost scarier than his loud anger.

"Tell me I'm wrong," I challenged.

"Not all men are the same. And you can't lump me in with your dad. I know that's what you're trying to do."

"No?" I asked. "If you're so different from him, why are you ditching me now that I'm pregnant?"

His eyes shot fire at me. "This is not the same!"

I laughed bitterly. "How is it different?"

"At least I'm offering you money!"

I wanted to argue, but Bryce jumped up and stormed out of the room before I could say anything else. A moment later, I heard the front door slam shut.

Bryce was gone.

I set the food tray on the floor next to the bed and turned onto my side, pulling the covers up to my chin.

I squeezed my eyes shut, wishing that I could wake up from the bad dream I was trapped in.

CHAPTER 25

BRYCE

*T*he only thing that never let me down was work.

I was damn good at what I did—not only did my dad teach me well, but I'd studied this stuff, and I had a knack for business. Besides, making money was clear-cut and simple. I knew what I needed to do, and taking things one step at a time offered results. There was nothing more to it.

When I buckled down and whittled away at a business problem, I was successful.

Unlike in a relationship, which was so damned hard it was impossible to understand. How much had I put into this whole thing? I'd done as Cora asked, *dating* her in the true sense of the word. I'd put my all into the marriage to bring us closer.

And it had. It had brought us so much closer.

And because of that, now that it was all falling apart, it was that much harder.

This was why I didn't date. This was why I didn't do anything more than one-night stands. The moment your fucking *feelings* got involved, everything got complicated.

I didn't need that shit in my life.

Cora was willing to cut me out of the equation completely. She was stubborn. And there was no doubt she could have a kid by herself if she wanted to. I had learned a lot about her in the past five months, and one thing was clear: she could bounce back from anything.

Plus, once she made up her mind about something, there was little that could throw her off.

That's why I knew that when she decided I wouldn't be in the picture, I couldn't change her mind. No matter what I said to her, or how hard I tried.

And she was adamant. She was going to have this baby herself. The fact that she'd thrown my money in my face—twice—just showed that she wasn't interested in a life with me after the agreement was over. Not even when we she was pregnant with my child.

Work gave me a break from obsessing about Cora. But all business days came to an end, and when it was time to go home, I couldn't bring myself to do it. I needed to get away. I couldn't face her yet.

Losing her hurt too much.

When I climbed in my car and drove off, my past seemed to pull at me, and I ended up in front of the Baron, a club that I used to go to all the time. It was an upper-class joint where the rich went to party, and social climbers went to prey on the rich.

I hadn't been here since the day before my dad hired Allison Evans, that PR manager, to get on my case about my image. Well, I bet she was fucking happy now—there hadn't been a bad article about me in the press for months.

I sat in the car for a moment, thinking. If I went in there, I was risking my standing with the board. I was risking everything.

But just because I was partying didn't mean I was a bad guy, right? I was allowed to have fun.

And fuck, I needed something to numb the pain.

I climbed out of my car and walked into the club, greeting the doormen and the waitresses who all knew me by name. I was taken to the VIP area right away, and I ended up with a scotch in my hand. Music thumped loudly all around me, and people moved their bodies to the beat.

And yet… this wasn't the distraction it used to be. For some reason, I couldn't get lost the way I used to. I couldn't forget about the rest of the world. Cora was still on my mind. And the baby.

I needed more to get my mind off things.

"Hey, handsome," a voice crooned close to my ear. I turned.

She was blonde, skinny, and her dress covered very little of her body.

"Do you want to dance with me?" She moved her body sensually to the beat of the music. The old me would have jumped at the opportunity to get her in bed.

But her long blonde hair only reminded me of Cora's blonde hair, and the way she moved wasn't as attractive as it used to be.

"I'm sorry," I said, shaking my head. "I'm married." I nearly choked on my own words. What the hell had come over me? Cora and I were married, but not because we loved each other. It was all a show. Technically, we could do whatever we wanted.

Except, it wasn't just a show anymore, was it? It was so much more than that.

She pouted and tried to convince me, but I shook my head and raised my hand for another scotch, throwing back the one I held in a smooth motion.

Another scotch arrived, and somewhere between sips, the

blonde disappeared, leaving me alone. That was better—I preferred to be alone.

I wasn't sure who this Bryce was, this new person. I didn't recognize him. This whole marriage had been designed to keep my position in the company. Six months of not sleeping around, and I could go right back to my playboy ways. That was the way I'd seen it.

But now, everything had changed. And once it was over, I had no idea who I would be.

All I knew was that I didn't want to do this alone. It was more than just care and concern for Cora and the baby.

It was love. I loved Cora, more than anything.

I'd been fooling myself into thinking that I could get over her, that it was a fling, that I'd just move on. What an idiot I was!

And as punishment for my own stupidity, I was about to lose her.

CHAPTER 26

*T*he gossip website's social media post was short and to the point. A brand-new picture of Bryce with a caption.

After months of absence, Bryce Hollis makes a grand entrance at the Baron. A leopard never changes his spots, right?

I clicked my phone off and closed my eyes, trying not to come undone at the seams.

That picture hit me so deep, I felt like throwing up. I knew Bryce and I weren't on good terms, but what the hell was he thinking?

Well, I knew the answer to that. He was thinking that he could do whatever the hell he wanted now that he and I were effectively over. Because that was what we were. Our agreement still had a little less than a month to go, but actions spoke a hell of a lot louder than words.

Bryce hadn't changed. I'd thought he'd grown up and realized he couldn't sleep his way through life. I'd thought what we had meant something to him.

Well, I'd been wrong. But this wouldn't be the first time. I'd been a poor judge of character before—my ex-boyfriends were proof enough of that. But then, I hadn't married any of them, had I? And I hadn't slept with them, either.

I'd been stupid enough to let Bryce convince me that he was different than other guys and that love could have a happy ending.

Well, none of that was true. He'd been a master actor. And now, after the article, I knew what was real.

The Bryce I'd read about countless times before. The man who used me to keep his job. That was real. The rest... wasn't.

When the front door banged open, I stiffened. I was curled up on the couch with a blanket. I'd been trying to watch a movie, although I'd struggled to concentrate. I'd started scrolling on my phone to distract myself, opening the tabloid app I hadn't had much time to look at lately.

When Bryce walked into the room, I could smell the smoke that clung to his clothes a mile away.

"Nice of you to come home. Alone," I said pointedly.

He looked at me with a frown. "What are you talking about?" There was alcohol on his breath. I didn't want to think about what else I'd smell on him if he came any closer.

"Did you have a good time at the club? The tabloids seem to think you're the prodigal son returned to his roots."

Bryce just blinked at me. I struggled to figure out just how drunk he was. Was he only tipsy? Or was he wasted? He'd always had a very good poker face.

This wasn't going to work. Partly because I was crazy in love with the guy, but he'd never stop going out and picking up women. I saw that now. And partly because I was having his baby and I wasn't going to sit at home with a child, hoping Bryce would come home in time to stay goodnight, to give our child a kiss that wasn't laced with alcohol.

Bryce wasn't father material.

We couldn't keep doing this.

"Look, we don't need to kid anyone anymore," I said when he still stared at me like he had no idea what I was talking about. "You and I aren't going to work. We're just—"

"No, Cora," Bryce said, cutting me off. "We're going to make this work. Us, the baby, all of it. We're going to make it happen."

I shook my head. "No."

"What?"

"I don't believe you," I said. I realized how honest I was being. With him, and with myself. "Why should I believe you? I care about you, Bryce, but you can't change your ways. You don't want to. I get that now."

"What would you know about what I want and don't want?"

"The proof is right here!" I cried out, pointing at my phone that lay on the couch. "You want the party life, and that's fine. I don't want someone in my life who won't put me and my baby first."

"Our baby."

"For all I know, it's just going to be me, Bryce. I don't see you stepping up and being the father figure you keep complaining you never had."

I knew it was wrong to keep bringing up his own family, but surely it had to count for something. He knew what it was like to grow up without a mom, with a detached dad. It made everything he was doing so much more unforgivable.

"Fine, you want to go there, let's go there," Bryce said. "What else about my life makes me so impossible to live with?"

"The fact that you will do whatever you need to put the company first. That should have been my first red flag, that the whole marriage was for the sake of the company."

"You knew that," Bryce said. "Don't act like I wasn't transparent with you. It's the baby that's a surprise, nothing else."

He had me there.

"You're right," I said. "But you don't care about me, Bryce. You won't change your ways for me and the baby, and that's where the problem lies. Without the women and clubs, you're all about business. All work and no play. Sal Hollis 2.0."

"That's not fair," Bryce said. He wasn't so drunk that he couldn't speak, that was clear. Maybe he was just tipsy. "You can't keep pointing fingers at my life without taking your own into account."

"What about my life?" My chest constricted.

"Your history with your dad makes it impossible for you to trust me. You just assumed I wouldn't be there for you and the baby."

"I didn't have to assume it!" I said. "You made it clear you were leaving me."

"I'm not leaving you, Cora," Bryce said, exasperated.

"No," I said tightly. "I'm leaving you."

The words shocked both of us, and for a moment, they hung in the air between us, as if not knowing which way to go. But I'd said them, and I was going to damn well follow through because it was the right thing to do. For me and for the baby.

I couldn't look at his face. I couldn't bear to see his reaction.

I got up, turned on my heel and stormed to the bedroom to get my things. I stuffed my phone, purse, and a few other items into a bag. My hands were shaking, and I could hardly think straight.

My vision blurred a few times as tears filled my eyes before spilling onto my cheeks. When I was finally done, I scrubbed angrily at my cheeks to erase the proof that I'd been crying and marched through the apartment.

Bryce wasn't in the living room where I'd left him. I faintly heard movement from his office.

I didn't go to him. What would I say? Instead, I walked to the front door and left.

It was only when I stepped into the lobby after riding down in the elevator that I realized he wasn't coming after me. Bryce wasn't going to try to stop me. He was going to let me walk out of his life without a word of protest.

And it wasn't until that moment that I realized I'd wanted him to. I'd hoped he would stop me, ask me to stay.

But he wasn't. And I wasn't going to turn around and crawl back with my tail between my legs.

I didn't have much, but I at least had my pride.

My hands were still shaking as I reached for my phone to call a cab. I was going home, and that would be the end of it. There was nothing left for me here.

Even if the man I loved was upstairs. With a bitter laugh, I realized he was probably working. Just as I expected he would. I'd come to know him well.

Despite everything, I'd come to love him.

But clearly, that wasn't enough to save us.

CHAPTER 27

BRYCE

*T*wo days. That was how long Cora was away before I realized that this was it.

It was over. She was gone for good.

I didn't know why it took me so long to understand that. Maybe because I'd kept hoping she would come back to me. Maybe because I'd hoped she would call and ask me if I would have her, if I could take her back.

My answer would have been yes, in a heartbeat. God, I missed having her around. I missed going out on silly dates and doing trivial little things just so that we could be together and get to know each other. I missed talking to her and laughing with her.

Everything in the apartment reminded me of her. It had become her home, too. Every corner, every piece of furniture, held a memory of Cora.

It was all wrong without her.

The doorman called me when I was home the next Saturday morning, and my heart leaped into my throat. Was it Cora? Did she want to see me?

I could have called her. It had crossed my mind a hundred

times to dial her number and hear her voice, to ask her if there was something we could save. But she was the one who had called it off, I kept telling myself. She was the one that had to come back if that was what she wanted. She would do it, if she really cared. She would come back to me.

That was what I kept convincing myself. It was easier than admitting that I was a coward.

The real reason I didn't call her was because I was scared she would tell me, again, that it was over.

I wasn't sure I could bear hearing it another time.

"A visitor for you, sir," the doorman said. "One Avery Jones."

I frowned. The name was familiar, but I couldn't place it. But then, my heart quickened when I remembered she was Cora's friend.

"Send her up," I said.

I went to the window to look out on the street below. Had Cora come with her? Maybe she was down on the street.

Anxiously, I waited in the foyer for the elevator doors to open. The young woman who stepped out had flame-red hair, and I recognized her from the wedding. Cora had mentioned she was an employee of mine, but I didn't know them all personally.

She blinked for a moment as she looked at me. She seemed overwhelmed. Then she forced herself to speak after a quick gulp of air.

"Mr. Hollis, hello."

"Is Cora with you?" I asked impatiently.

"No, no. She's not here."

I sighed.

"She sent me here," Avery said. "To get her things."

I nearly choked. "Her things?"

Avery swallowed. "Yeah, she left behind some clothes. She described it all to me and asked me to come get it for her."

"Let me get this straight. You want me to let you into my apartment?"

"Or I could tell you what all she needs, and you could get it?" She scrunched up her face pleadingly.

I shook my head. "If Cora wants her stuff, tell her she can come get it herself. I'm not playing these games."

Avery nodded uncomfortably. "I'll let her know, Mr. Hollis." She turned toward the elevator.

I furrowed my brow as reality sunk in. Cora was finished with me. She wasn't coming back. And she didn't even want to see me one last time.

Avery got on the elevator, but I barely noticed. I was left standing in the foyer in a daze.

Our agreement ended in under four weeks, but Cora couldn't stand to be with me for another minute.

The floor became unstable beneath my feet. The room spun slowly, and I felt lightheaded.

Cora wanted to get rid of me.

I hadn't expected to feel so ripped apart. I hadn't expected for the news to tear me apart. But it did. In fact, it was like a knife to the heart. I had the physical chest pains to prove it.

This was all wrong. I'd thought we would resolve our issues. I'd thought we would get through it.

I'd been wrong.

I found my phone and dialed Cora's number. I just had to talk to her, to get through this without involving anyone else. I wanted to speak to her, personally.

The phone rang and rang and finally rolled over to voicemail.

I cursed under my breath and tried again. And another time.

Nothing.

Maybe it looked desperate that I was calling over and over. But I didn't care about my pride anymore.

I went downstairs and climbed in my car. I drove to the one place I knew to find her. If only she would speak to me. Even if it meant she would tell me to my face that it was really over, instead going through her friend. I just wanted it to be between me and her.

I walked to the front door when I arrived at the Rhodes residence, and my heart beat in my throat when I raised a fist to knock. I hesitated, terrified of what I was going to find on the other side of that door. But I couldn't just let her leave, no matter how scared I was.

I knocked.

After a moment I heard footsteps on the other side of the door, and then it opened.

Rachel stood in front of me.

"Bryce," she said in a gentle voice, but I didn't know how to read her expression. Did she hate me? What had Cora said about me? Could Rachel be on my side, somehow?

"Is Cora here?" I asked in a hoarse voice.

Rachel shook her head no. She looked much better than when I'd seen her last—stronger, healthier. Her cheeks were rosy and her eyes were sharp. Compared to the first night we'd met, she was a different woman.

"Come in," Rachel said. "Let me get you coffee. You look like you need it."

I needed something much stronger than coffee, but I stepped into the house and followed Rachel to the kitchen, where she put on a fresh pot. While it brewed, I looked around, trying to imagine Cora living here once more. Would it be enough for her, after she'd lived so differently? Or had she been yearning to return to this simpler life all along?

When my eyes fell on Rachel, I realized she'd been watching me.

"You're upset," she said.

I nodded. "She wants to end it."

Rachel didn't look surprised by this. Cora must have told her everything.

"You don't?" Rachel asked.

I took a deep breath and let it out slowly. "I don't want it to end like this."

Rachel nodded. "She's scared to death, you know. Of having this baby."

Cora had told her about that, too, then.

"I know it's a big deal, but—"

"You have no idea what a big deal it is to her," Rachel interrupted me. "She grew up without a father, and I taught her never to rely on a man. I also warned her never to end up where I was. And yet…"

"It's exactly the same," I said.

Rachel shook her head. "Not quite the same, I can see that. You care about her, don't you?"

I nodded. "I don't always know how to show it."

"You're reluctant to be open—because you're protecting yourself, I assume. But it comes across like you're indifferent."

I tried to process what this meant. Could it be that by being too careful, I'd just made Cora think I was pushing her away?

Rachel poured us each a cup of coffee when the machine finished and we walked to the living room. I couldn't help but notice all the framed pictures of Cora on the wall—from infancy to high school. She had always been adorable.

"For a long time, Cora believed her father left because of her," Rachel said.

"Why would she think that? Her father never met her, right?" I asked.

Rachel shrugged. "She figured that everything was fine between me and her father until I came along. Of course, it wasn't like that. But he decided to leave when I was pregnant with her. So she always blamed herself. She thought if she'd never come along…"

"I see," I said, nodding. I was starting to understand what she was so scared of. Me leaving, raising the child on her own, not being good enough. Repeating history. If only she knew how good she was, if only she could see herself through my eyes.

"When I look at Cora," I said, staring into my cup of coffee, "I see someone who's willing to help others, no matter how bad things are in her own life. She's selfless and caring and compassionate in a way that very few people are. That makes her rare. And precious. Like a gem."

Rachel nodded. "I've always known that my little girl would be amazing one day. And I've hoped and prayed that she would find someone who would see that light in her, not do what they could to snuff it out. I'll be truthful. I didn't think much of you when I met you, Bryce. But so far, you've surprised me."

"That's good to hear," I said. "If only Cora could see it that way." My eyes drifted to a photo of Cora as a young child with blonde pigtails. She had a big grin, and she was missing her two front teeth. Even as a little girl, she had that sparkle in her eye I loved so much today.

I realized what I wanted to do. I wanted Cora back. I needed to make this right. I wanted to give her the life she deserved and wipe away all her worries and her fears.

Because she was incredible. She was everything I needed in my life, and I wanted to be everything I could be for her. She inspired me to be a better version of myself. I hated that she thought I was like her father, and that her history was doomed to repeat itself.

I would show her otherwise. I would prove to her what she meant to me.

I'd married her for the sake of my company, but I'd realized in the past months that there was so much more to life than just work. And she had become more important to me than anything. Even if I hadn't realized it at first.

I knew it now. I knew beyond a shadow of a doubt that Cora was the woman for me.

CHAPTER 28

CORA

I couldn't let heartbreak get me down.

And my heart was broken, terribly. I sobbed in my mother's arms and then went to my room and cried more. I was in pain, and nothing helped.

I'd fallen in love with Bryce. I'd tried not to, but it had happened anyway. And he didn't even care about me.

But I had to look toward the future and get my plans figured out. I was going to be a mother soon. And single—a divorcée, once the divorce went through. Just saying those words seemed bizarre.

Getting married, falling in love, and heading toward divorce had all happened so fast. I was reeling.

But right now, I was taking things one step at a time.

The first issue was that I was still a month shy of the six-month marriage agreement. Which meant that even though I'd told Bryce to keep the money, I wasn't getting it now. I'd forfeited three million dollars by walking out early.

It might not have been my best move.

I wouldn't have accepted it, though. Not after he told me that I was a gold digger and just wanted his money. Not after he accused me of trying to wiggle my way into his bank account permanently by getting pregnant on purpose. I wasn't like that, and I resented the fact that he'd accused me of it.

I would work with what I had.

I had a huge rock on my finger—my wedding ring was expensive as hell. That would pull me through for a while. I was going to sell it and set up what I could for the baby. I was going to have to figure this out alone, so I would do my best to hit the ground running. My mom would be there to help me out, and that was better than nothing.

But she'd already raised one child alone. I wasn't going to expect anything from her other than being a loving grandmother. She needed to heal still, too. Plus, she was ready to start working, and it looked like she would do so in the next month. At least that was a bit of a load off—it would be another income to help out, and that would make a big difference.

Soon, I'd have to get a new job. I couldn't keep working at Hollis Marketing.

But first, I had to get the rest of my things from the penthouse.

When I left, I'd been so upset I couldn't pack everything. Now, I needed that stuff. My clothes, toiletries, personal items—I couldn't afford to replace it all. Plus, maybe I could sell some of the dresses and bags he'd bought me.

Surely, he wouldn't hold it against me if I took the clothes he'd bought me. I needed some cash until I could figure out a way to permanently support us—including the baby.

I chose Monday morning to go to the apartment. Avery had told me about her brief meeting with Bryce. So he knew I was calling it off, which meant he would be burying himself at the office. He'd be looking for a way to do damage control in case any of the tabloids discovered I'd moved out.

He clearly cared more about his reputation than me. But I knew he wouldn't lose his position as CEO. The board of directors had been won over, and they weren't going to throw him out. And I knew that had a lot to do with my acting as his wife.

When I arrived at the penthouse, the doorman let me up as if I still lived there. A pang shot through my heart, but I pushed it firmly away and marched on. I had to get through this without getting too emotional.

I opened the door and stepped into the penthouse suite that had once been my home and closed the door behind me.

Bryce stood in the middle of the living room as if he'd been waiting for me, and I froze.

"You're here," I said breathlessly. "I…" I wasn't sure what to say.

"Yeah," Bryce said. "I'm here. I knew you'd come back at least one more time before you walked away completely."

I swallowed hard, trying to breathe around the lump that was rising in my throat.

"I'm just here to pick up a few things," I said, clearing my throat.

"Cora," Bryce said, taking a step closer.

I stopped and blinked at him. If he said anything now that wasn't cruel, I'd break down and cry. I half-hoped he would say something mean so that I could use anger to get through this, but his face was gentle and kind, his eyes filled with emotion, and he didn't look like he wanted to pick a fight at all.

"This arrived in the mail today," he announced, reaching for a large envelope on the coffee table.

I squinted at the return address. A chill went down my spine when I recognized the name of the law firm. They were the divorce papers.

"They sent them a few weeks early, just like we arranged when we set this whole thing up," he said.

I swallowed the lump forming in my throat. I'd forgotten those were due to arrive already.

Bryce turned the envelope onto its side and looked at me. He tore the entire thing in half.

I gasped.

He put the two halves together and tore it down the middle another time before he tossed it to the side.

Then, he dropped to one knee.

"What are you doing?" I asked, confused.

"Cora, forgive me. I fucked up so bad. I know you'd never try to steal my money. I'm sorry I accused you of that. I lied when I said I was ready for it to be over." He shook his head. "I let my pride get in the way. I thought you didn't care for me, and I couldn't show how much I love you. I couldn't let you know how much it hurt to lose you. Then I went to that stupid club, but I didn't even look at another woman. You're all I want, Cora. You and this baby."

My eyes stung with tears. I had the urge to pinch myself. "Did you say you love me?"

He squeezed my hands. "Yes, Cora. I love you so much. I want to spend my life with you. For real. Marry me."

"We're already married," I said in a thick voice. Tears rolled over my cheeks, and I was irritated with myself for not being able to hold it all in. But he was on his knee, proposing the way he never had when we started this whole thing.

I knew he was speaking the truth. This was the real Bryce. I'd known him all along.

"I know," he said. "But I didn't do this part. I didn't do it right. You deserve to know how precious and beautiful and important you are. And how much I need you. I want to do this with you. I'm done acting. I'm done hiding my true feelings. I want to be your real husband. And I want to be a father to this child."

He pressed his face against my belly and planted a kiss there.

I blinked through my tears at the man who stood on one knee in front of me and wondered how this was happening. I was getting the fairy tale I never knew I wanted. But now that Bryce was here in front of me, pouring his heart out to me, I knew that being with him was exactly what I wanted.

This was where I belonged.

"Yes," I whispered.

Bryce looked up at me with surprise.

"I'll marry you," I said, my face opening up into a smile. "I love you, Bryce."

He was frozen for a moment, as if he hadn't expected me to say yes. But then he jumped up and grabbed me, pulling me tightly against him into a hug. He lifted me off the ground and spun me around as I yelped and laughed.

He covered my face in kisses, and I never wanted it to stop.

"Oh, Bryce," I murmured.

"I can't believe I almost lost you," he said. "Or how stubborn you are."

I giggled. "How stubborn we *both* are."

"That's for sure. But no more, Cora. No more hiding behind my pride."

"And no more hiding our true feelings," I added.

He held my body against his, and it felt wonderful. We were together again, his arms wrapped tightly around me. No matter how hard I worked or how strong I was, no matter that I could do this on my own, having Bryce by my side was just that much better.

When he let go of me again, he beamed at me. His eyes slid to my stomach, and I fought the urge to cover up. This wasn't something I needed to hide anymore. Bryce and I were going to have a baby.

Together.

"How far along are you?" he asked.

I shook my head. "I'm not sure. But I think it's far. About three months." I swallowed. "I didn't realize until the other day. I didn't plan it. I'm just usually irregular and—"

"And it means we just have a few more months to wait for our little boy or girl to join us on this adventure."

Bryce carefully slid his hand onto my belly, which had gotten bigger even in the past few days. I was really starting to show now.

"I can't wait for this new chapter in our lives," he said.

"Really?" I asked. "You're not... terrified?"

"I am," he admitted. "But I'm not going anywhere. We're doing this together, okay?"

I let out a breath.

"No matter how scary this is," he continued, "it's you and me together. And I can tell you now, my dad is going to be ecstatic to know he's going to be a grandfather."

I beamed. "My mom was crazy happy, too. Even though she was worried about me."

"She doesn't have to worry anymore," Bryce said. "It's you and me, babe. We're a team."

He kissed me, and I melted against him. I couldn't believe that after all the pain and heartache, the uncertainty and difficulty, I could ever be this happy. I couldn't believe that despite this whole thing being an act for the board members, I had found the man I wanted to spend the rest of my life with.

"I love you, Cora," Bryce said, breaking the kiss to look at me.

I smiled at him. "I love you, Bryce."

He grinned at me before he gave me another quick kiss.

"We have work to do," he said.

"What work?"

"We have to get your stuff back in here so your closet isn't so empty. I hate not having you around here." He paused. "That is, if you're ready to come back."

I nodded and smiled. "Absolutely."

Bryce grabbed his keys and headed for the door.

"Now?" I asked.

"Now," Bryce said. "Besides, we need to tell your mom the good news."

I laughed. Bryce was so excited now that we were officially back together again. It was endearing. He took my hand and led me to the elevator. As we rode to the first floor, he interlinked his fingers with mine and lifted my hand to his mouth, brushing his lips against my knuckles.

I leaned in against him and sighed.

I felt light and airy, as if a weight had dropped from my shoulders. For the past few months, I'd been deliriously happy. But I had always known this deadline would creep closer, and that at some point, it would all come to an end.

Now, I didn't have to worry anymore. I loved Bryce, and he felt the same about me. The agreement, the deadline, all of it was gone. We were going to be together forever.

I didn't know what the future held for us. I wasn't sure what would happen with my job now that I was pregnant. But we would figure it all out.

I could finally lay my history to rest. I had Bryce, and he wasn't going anywhere. Together, we'd rewrite the story with a happier ending, a family that was beautiful and complete, and a future that was bright and wonderful. It was all just waiting for us.

CHAPTER 29

BRYCE

*A*fter we collected all the things from Rachel's home that belonged back at the penthouse—and we all cried together again when Cora told her mom that we were going to make it work—we went back home. Our home.

We sat on the couch together in the living room and looked out at the dusk that was falling over LA.

Cora's legs were thrown causally over mine, but her body was tilted slightly away and her mind was spinning—I could practically see the cogs turning as she thought long and hard about things I wasn't privy to.

I studied her profile in the growing darkness, her raw beauty. When she was made up for the board meetings or the cocktail parties, she looked incredible, but she had a natural beauty about her that shone through from the inside.

I would never get tired of staring at her. Her high cheek-bones, her perfect nose, the slim arches of her brows.

But she had a frown on her face. Whatever she was thinking seemed troubling.

"Penny for your thoughts?" I asked.

She glanced at me, her eyes filled with concern and fear. I

didn't like to see those emotions on her face. I wanted to make them go away.

"I was just thinking about us."

"And you don't look happy."

"No, I am," she said quickly, reaching for my face and touching it. "I'm happier than ever. But…"

She hesitated, and I almost cringed, waiting for the blow. A 'but' was never a good thing.

"What?" I asked cautiously.

"You're not settling for me, are you?"

My heart constricted. "Are you kidding me?"

She looked up at me, quiet. I sat up and turned to look her in the eye.

"Cora, being with you could never be called settling. I love you. All I want is you."

She smiled slightly. "I love you, too, Bryce. But we're talking about a totally different lifestyle here. For both of us, but especially you. Settling down permanently… Well, it'll be a big change from the nightclubs."

I chuckled and took her hands in mine. "I don't want that life anymore. I only went to the club the other night because I was destroyed over losing you. I thought I could fool myself into forgetting you by going back to my old way of life. But there was nothing for me there. Nothing at all."

She chewed on her lip, thinking.

"That party guy I used to be? He's long gone. And good riddance. I like myself much better now," I said.

"Really?"

"Really. Cora, you've changed my life for the better in so many ways. You've changed me. My dad and I have gotten closer because of you. I'm better at my job. I'm not going through life with a chip on my shoulder anymore. You've made me a better man."

Her eyes lit up. "You've made me a better woman, too."

I smiled. "You don't have to worry, Cora. That old way of living is dead to me now. So meaningless. I can't imagine returning to it. Now that I know what real love is, there's no going back."

That seemed to satisfy her. And it was the truth. I had no interest in being LA's notorious playboy anymore.

"And you're ready to take on fatherhood?"

"Well, not quite today. But I do have a few more months to prepare, don't I?"

She laughed. "I need that time, too. God, I can't believe I'm going to be a mom!"

I kissed her forehead. "You're going to be a great mom."

She settled in against my chest once more. "I think it's going to be fun."

"Me, too. It'll be a learning curve. But if we stick together, we'll do just fine."

She sighed happily. "I love you."

"I love you, too."

We were quiet for a while. Then, she ran her hand along my thigh, slowly, teasingly. It was unexpected, but it made my cock stiffen right away. She turned around and climbed into my lap, straddling me. I moved my hands around her waist as she leaned in to kiss me. Her soft lips pressed against mine, and I breathed in her intoxicating scent. Her mouth parted, letting me into her soft wetness. Then she pulled back to look at me with hooded eyes.

"Bryce," she whispered. "I want you."

I looked in her eyes, deep and shining in the darkness of the room.

"I'm all yours," I answered.

I pushed my hand into her hair and kissed her again, sliding my tongue over her lips before she broke the kiss. She stood up, took my hand, and led me to the main bedroom. As soon as we were on the bed, she pressed her body against mine. I could feel the swells of her breasts through her thin dress, and she threw one leg over mine, feeling my erection against her thigh. She couldn't miss it—I was turned on as fuck.

She moved her leg up and down, pressing herself up against my sex. I knew how much she wanted this.

Just as much as I wanted her.

I slid my hand down the side of her body, feeling the curve of her breast, the dip of her narrow waist. I grazed my hand along her thigh, holding her more firmly, grinding myself against her. I slid my hand to her ass and squeezed. She grabbed at my shirt, pulling it over my head and running her hands over my chest.

It had only been a short while without her, but God, I'd missed her. I'd missed this. Being so close to each other that we were practically one and the same.

I loved the feel of her body against mine, the way she moved, gasping and moaning into my mouth.

Cora shifted, pulling herself on top of me. She unbuckled my belt and pulled my pants down, and I kicked them off. She straddled me, her pussy against my cock. She wasn't wearing any panties, and only the thin material of my boxers separated us. She moved her hips, riding me slowly, and I groaned.

I was getting harder and harder, and I needed her. I wanted to be inside of her.

"You're so fucking hot," I whispered to her, staring at her, hoping she could see the lust in my eyes.

Cora lowered and pressed her lips against mine. She lifted her hips a little, and pushing her hand into my boxers, pulled my cock free. Her fingers slid up and down my shaft while she kissed me—our tongues swirled together and my breathing was getting ragged—and she pumped her hand up and down, faster and faster.

"Oh, God, Cora," I groaned. It was incredible. She was great with her hands. But I wanted more.

I'd barely thought it when she broke the kiss, let go of my sex, and started kissing her way down my neck and onto my chest. She ran her hands over my chest, my abs, and shifted her body onto my thighs as she worked her way down.

I'd never felt as complete with anyone as I did with Cora. The thought of a permanent commitment would have scared the hell out of me months ago. Now, it made me feel like I'd finally done something right. I'd fought for the woman I loved instead of letting her go.

I gasped when Cora sucked my cock into her mouth. At first, it was just the head, but she swirled her tongue around it. I shivered and jerked, my body responding to her advances.

She curled her fingers around the waistband of my boxers and pulled them down.

She sank her head down, sucking my cock deep into her mouth. My head pushed against the back of her throat, and she rolled her eyes up to look at me.

Holy fuck.

She started pumping her head up and down. I moaned, pushing my hands into her hair to encourage her, guide her. But she didn't need help. She knew exactly what she was doing, and if she continued like that, she was going to push me over the edge long before I wanted any of this to be over.

Suddenly, she sat up, my cock falling out of her mouth with a plop. She looked at me, her eyes filled with hunger and need that echoed my own.

She reached for her dress, her arms crossed over her body, and she pulled the material up and over her head.

In one movement, she was completely naked.

I stared at her perfect body—her milky skin, the swells of her breasts, her dark, erect nipples. The way her body dipped at her waist and widened around her perfect hips. And the slight belly she'd developed lately, that I now knew was filled with a growing life.

She was carrying my baby.

Suddenly, I was overcome by emotion. This was bigger than anything I could have imagined.

I waited for the fear to set in, for the worry about being tied down for the rest of my life to take over as it had before.

But it didn't come. Instead, I was overwhelmed by a sense of amazement, knowing that this was my future and being perfectly happy with it.

I had no idea what was going to happen once this baby was born. I hadn't planned on being a father at all—when my life was a series of one-night stands, plans for my future were comprised of nothing more than having birth control at hand and being prepared for a hell of a hangover the next morning.

But with Cora, I wanted it all. The future, the plans, the uncertainty of what was to come and the knowledge that we were going to find out together.

"Are you okay?" Cora asked, her brow furrowed. I'd been staring at her for a while, and I wasn't sure what my face had shown.

I looked at her and smiled, nodding. I took her hands.

"I'm okay," I said. "More than okay."

I pulled her closer to me, kissing her. But this wasn't just a kiss filled with lust and need. I poured everything I felt into her and wrapped my arms around her naked body.

She was all I wanted.

CHAPTER 30

CORA

*S*omething was different about the way Bryce kissed me. But it was a good kind of different. It was warm and emotional. It was perfect.

He kissed me like he meant it, like I was everything to him. Like I was his whole world.

I had never felt so incredibly special, so wanted.

After everything that had gone wrong between us, it was almost impossible to imagine that so much had suddenly gone right. Just this morning, I had been planning to do it all by myself. And I had been broken after losing Bryce.

But now, with our naked bodies pressed tightly together, the way Bryce kissed me made me think that this was about more than sex. It was deeper, more emotional, more real.

He shifted while I was on top of him, positioned his erection at my entrance, and I held my breath in anticipation.

When he slid inside me, we gasped in unison. We came together as one, and it was more than just pure sexual pleasure that washed through me. It was the connection, the togetherness, the oneness between us.

We were so close together, and it wasn't just physically.

Emotionally, we were closer than ever. So close that as I lay on top of him with his cock buried inside of me, I didn't know where he ended and I began.

After a long time just being together this way, with him inside of me, the two of us melded together, Bryce started moving.

I helped him, moving my hips, sliding him in and out of me with small movements.

He pulled back his arms, and I pushed up on his chest so that I was sitting on top of him. I trembled with need, and started rocking my hips backward and forward, feeling him slide in and out, going deeper and deeper with every thrust. I rocked harder and faster, letting my need for him take over, and my clit rubbed against his pubic bone. The motion, the friction against my G-spot, and the way I was rubbing up against him pushed me closer and closer to the edge.

An orgasm erupted inside of me, and I cried out, tilted forward. My hair fell over my face, and I hung my head as I let the pleasure take over. It washed over me, making my body clamp down on Bryce's cock. I was filled with pure, unadulterated pleasure, and I leaned heavily on Bryce's chest, trying to keep my balance.

I collapsed when the orgasm subsided, breathing hard, gasping.

Bryce chuckled and the deep, velvety sound of his voice rumbled through his chest.

He flipped me over, rolling with me in one smooth movement, and before I knew what was happening, he was on top and buried deep inside me again.

"I love it when you do that," he said in a soft voice.

"What?" I gasped, trying to relearn how to breathe.

"Lose yourself in pleasure."

I didn't have a chance to respond. Bryce started sliding in

and out of me, slowly at first, and I gasped in rhythm with him.

As he moved his hips faster and faster, he started thrusting into me deeper. I cried out and moaned his name, gripping his shoulders, holding on for dear life as he moved inside me.

I'd needed this. I'd needed us to be grounded in what we felt for each other. Bryce and I were a lot more than just sex. Choosing him as my first lover had been the right thing to do. But we were together in another way, too. Connected, on the same page, emotionally.

And this sex, the intense lovemaking that drove me crazy every time, only sealed the deal.

It almost felt like this was the first time after our wedding, the consummation of our marriage. Because even though every other time had been fantastic, and I'd become attached to Bryce in a way I'd never expected, this was the way it was meant to be.

This was what it was like when two people became one.

Bryce gritted his teeth and fucked me harder, his strokes shortening, and I knew he was close. He let out a sharp cry and pushed into me as deeply as he could.

I felt him jerking and spasming as he emptied himself inside of me, and it was incredible. An echo of my own orgasm returned and we rode out the wave of ecstasy together.

The pleasure, the bliss, took a long time to subside. When it finally did, Bryce dropped his head into my neck, nuzzling his nose against my skin. He was breathing hard. So was I.

He slipped out of me a moment later, already softening, and collapsed on the bed. We were both gasping, lying next to each other. Bryce reached for me and took my hand, interlinking our fingers.

I loved it when he held onto me like that, as if he was

worried I would float away. As if he wanted to keep me here forever.

Well, I would be here forever.

Bryce reached for the tissues on the nightstand and handed them to me. I smiled at the face I'd come to love, the face I was sure I could wake up to for the rest of my life and never, ever get bored of.

He held out his arm and I shifted, moving into his embrace. He wrapped his arm around my shoulder, and I wriggled even closer—as close as I could get.

Happiness flooded my body. I finally knew that he loved me. Our relationship was real, at long last.

Yesterday, I didn't know how I would cope without him. I had a hollow inside of me that craved being filled, and the only person that could fill that emptiness was Bryce. I had never known that I needed him until I met him. I'd been perfectly happy alone, but now that I knew what life was like with him, being without him felt wrong.

Hearing him declare his love for me and propose marriage—real marriage—had been the sweetest words I'd ever heard. Now, I was back in his arms where I belonged.

And God, the sex was fantastic. Not just because Bryce was damn good in bed, but because we'd come together in a deeper way than ever before. It had healed us.

I lay with my head on his chest, feeling his heartbeat against my cheek. The rhythm was steady, his chest rising and falling with his breathing.

For a moment, I thought he was asleep, but then he shifted slightly.

"I have something for you," he said with a grin.

I sat up so he could get out of bed and he padded butt-naked out of the room. I giggled as I watched him go. When he came back, he had a small black box in his hand.

I frowned. "What is that?"

"It's for you," he said, and climbed onto the bed again, giving me the box. "I didn't get a chance to give it to you earlier."

I flipped it open and gasped. It was a diamond ring. But nothing like the gaudy one I wore on my finger for the sake of the tabloids. This one was more tasteful, elegantly designed. It was clear a lot of thought had gone into it.

"Bryce…" I said, not knowing how to continue.

"Do you like it?"

"It's beautiful," I breathed. It was exactly what I would have chosen for myself. He'd gotten to know what I liked and what was important to me.

He'd seen the real me.

I looked at him. He pulled me in close for a kiss.

"Thank you," I said. "My husband."

"Always," he said. "Everything for you. My wife."

I smiled again and took the other ring off, sliding the new one onto my finger. It looked amazing.

This was the start of something new, something real. This time, it wasn't a sham. Bryce and I were together because we chose to be, because we wanted to be in each other's lives. For no other reason than because we loved each other.

Bryce lay down again, and I shifted under the covers, wrapping my body around his. He reached over, switched off the lamp on the nightstand, and plunged the room into darkness.

My eyes adjusted, the shapes in the room becoming clearer, and I glanced toward the curtains that were drawn. Out there lay a city with twinkling lights, my home, and I was in the penthouse of a tall building, looking out over it. The symbolism wasn't lost on me. I was at the top of the world, and my future was stretched out in front of me, beautiful and enticing.

I let my hand slide over my lower belly. This baby was

already so loved. And soon, he or she was going to join us. Now that everything was perfect, I couldn't wait to have this baby. The life growing inside me symbolized the love we shared. It was the product of two people coming together and being exactly right, fitting together as if they were made for each other.

That was us—perfect together. And perfectly happy in this new life we'd created.

I sighed contentedly and closed my eyes. Bryce's arm curled tighter around me, pulling me against him.

Tomorrow would bring a new chapter, a new life. We were going to take on the world like this—side by side.

EPILOGUE

CORA

Fourteen months later

The sound of Zoe's squeals over the baby monitor woke me up, and I stretched under the sheets. Next to me, Bryce shifted and yawned.

"I'm going to get her," I said.

"Bring her here," he answered.

I nodded, planted a quick kiss on his lips, and slipped out of bed. I walked across the hall to the nursery. Bryce and I had redecorated the room after we'd gone to my first ultrasound together and found out we were expecting a baby girl.

I pushed the door open to soft pink walls with gray cartoon elephants picking flowers on them.

Zoe's chubby little cheeks grinned at me when I saw her in her crib.

"There's my little girl!" I crooned and hurried to her.

Her short blonde hair, as golden as mine, was a mess after sleeping, and her green eyes were filled with laughter. Her chubby little arms reached up to me.

"Come here, honey." I hoisted her out of the crib and

nuzzled her neck, cuddling her little body to mine. She gripped my hair with both hands and tugged.

"Oh, that's Mommy's hair," I laughed, trying to pry her fingers open with one hand while I held her.

When she wouldn't let go, I put her down on the changing table so I could use both hands. She squealed and blew spit bubbles at me, her mouth curled into a permanent smile. She hadn't stopped since the day she'd figured out how.

"Did you have a good night, angel face?" I spoke softly while I changed her. "You look like you had a good night. And today's a fun day! Today is a new beginning."

I finished changing her and dressed her again. When I was done, I blew raspberries on her cheeks and she squealed and giggled.

"Come on, Daddy's waiting."

I carried her to the main bedroom. When we walked in, Bryce sat up in bed.

"There's my little princess," he said and held out his arms. I handed her over, and he cuddled her. She lay on her back and kicked her feet.

I looked at Bryce over our daughter, and my heart swelled with pride and joy. It had been eight months since Zoe was born. That little girl had burst both our hearts wide open.

Bryce and I were better than ever. For a while, I had been nervous that things would change, that having a baby would alter our dynamic. Since we hadn't been together long, it could have made things harder.

There were days that were tough. There were misunderstandings and exhaustion from sleepless nights.

But we worked through it. There were no more nightclubs or threats to leave. Neither of us doubted the other's commitment.

And I was happier than I had ever been.

"So, are you ready for today?" I asked.

Bryce grinned at me. "Definitely ready."

We stayed in bed for a while longer, playing with Zoe, making her giggle and laugh. Bryce was amazing with her—he was dedicated to spoiling her rotten, and I had never seen a more involved father.

For two people who came from broken homes, I figured we were doing okay. And Bryce was doing an amazing job being here for me and Zoe, doting on his family first and foremost.

The company was important to him. He was well past his probationary period and was bringing the business to new heights as CEO. But he put us first. Always.

When it was time to get up, Bryce carried Zoe to the kitchen to set her up in her seat and start on breakfast. I hopped in the shower, and by the time I joined them, Bryce had pancakes going and Zoe was elbows deep in a bowl of baby cereal.

"Oh, my," I said and hurried to her, grabbing a cloth to mop up what I could. "You didn't see this?" I asked.

"Of course I saw it," Bryce said with a grin. "But I was just as messy with the pancake batter. And we should all have some fun in the kitchen."

I laughed. Bryce was such a relaxed father.

We ate together—Bryce and I had scrambled eggs, bacon, and pancakes. After her baby cereal, I gave Zoe some pieces of banana.

Once we'd cleaned up after breakfast, the doorbell rang.

"Right on time," I said and carried Zoe to the door.

"Say hi to Grandma!" I said when I opened it, and my mom stretched out her arms, taking Zoe from me.

"Hello, my sweetheart," she said, kissing Zoe all over until the girl squealed.

My mom laughed, and I watched her with my daughter.

She looked good—she'd beaten the cancer completely. She'd gotten a totally clean bill of health at her last checkup. She was fresh and healthy and getting fitter again. She worked and loved her job, and I didn't need to worry about her anymore.

I'd also come clean to her about Bryce and the initially fake nature of our marriage. I hadn't wanted to lie anymore. After the initial shock wore off, we shared a big laugh about it.

"Where's that lovely husband of yours?" Mom asked.

"In the shower by now, I hope," I said. "We'll see you at the chapel."

"Good luck, Cora. I know you'll be great."

Mom kissed me goodbye and left with Zoe and a bag with her things, and I closed the door behind them.

I walked back to the bedroom, heard Bryce in the shower, and wished I could join him. But we had to get a move on.

I opened my closet and took out the white dress I'd bought. It was a simple dress in a soft material, with a scooped neckline, an open back, and a simple A-line skirt that fell to the floor. I grabbed the pearl purse I'd bought to match the jewelry and the shoes.

"Okay, I'm going!" I called out, not wanting him to catch a glimpse of the dress. It was silly, but I didn't care. "I love you."

"I'll see you there," Bryce called through the door. "Love you too!"

Avery was waiting for me in the lobby when I came down.

"You look fantastic," she said and hugged me. "I can't believe this is happening!"

"Me neither," I said and we walked outside, getting into the sleek black car Bryce had organized for us. We rode to the chapel, where a separate room had been set up for us to have our hair and makeup done, with champagne and a photographer to capture the whole thing.

I was nervous. I had no idea why—this wasn't nearly as intense as the wedding had been the first time around. But this time, it was serious. This time, it was real.

Time flew by. My hair and makeup were done, leaving time to drink champagne with my best friend. Finally, it was time to go.

We walked to the foyer, and Sal waited there for me. He was going to walk me down the aisle this time.

"Hello," he said with a grin. "You look fantastic."

"Thank you. You don't look so bad yourself."

"I clean up well." He winked, and I laughed.

He held his arm out for me, and when the music started, the bridesmaids walked in first.

Sal and I followed.

Bryce waited for me at the altar, and I smiled when I saw him. The man who had become my everything. His eyes were filled with affection.

The ceremony was a small one. My mom, Bryce's dad, a handful of our friends, and Zoe. That was it. It wasn't extravagant, it wasn't a public affair. It was private and intimate and just the way I wanted it.

When it was time to say our vows, they were personalized this time.

"Cora," Bryce started with his, "you taught me how to love when I was sure I would never learn how. Thank you for teaching me what life is really about. It's not about money and power—it's about making your loved ones happy. Learning that changed me forever. Cora, you are the light of my life, the love I never saw coming. If I can wake up to your face for the rest of my days, I will have reached the pinnacle of success and happiness. I love you, and I promise to cherish you forever."

My eyes welled with tears.

"Bryce," I said when it was my turn, "you came out of nowhere, a knight in shining armor, a hero. I was drowning, and you saved me in more ways than one. You taught me that trust and friendship complement love, and you showed me how to open my heart when it had been closed for too long. You've helped me to heal, and you've given me a family I never dreamed I'd have. I promise to be by your side, to be your devoted wife, no matter what. I love you."

The priest smiled. "And now," he said, "after this beautiful renewal of vows, you may celebrate with a kiss."

Bruce pulled me closer and kissed me, wrapping his arms around my waist. I threw my arms around his neck. Everyone cheered.

When we broke the kiss, I reached for Zoe and took her, and Bryce kissed her on the head.

"This is it," he said to me. "This is the fairy tale that I was sure didn't exist."

"It finally came true for us. This is the part where we ride off into the sunset," I agreed with a smile.

He glanced at me. "I don't know about you, but I can't wait for the rest of our lives together."

"I can't either, Bryce," I said. "You're my everything."

He leaned over and kissed me again.

As I looked at the small gathering, I smiled. Of all the people that could be with us, these were the people I cherished the most, the people I wanted to share our special day with. It was perfect and complete.

Then, I turned back to my husband and our daughter. The two loves of my life. My family, my whole world.

My heart was so full.

Bryce's eyes met mine, and I saw all the love I felt reflected back on me.

At that moment, there was nothing more real in the

world.

Thank you for reading Boss's Pretend Wife.

If you liked this book, you'll love **Come Back to Me!**

It's an irresistible story of second chances and a love that never quit. The happily ever after will leave you swooning!

Click here to get Come Back to Me now!

Here's a sneak peek:

Ten years ago Gavin broke my heart and my cherry.
Never saw him again.
Until I showed up to work today.

I built mile-high walls around my heart.
If he thinks he can parade his chiseled abs around
and make me fall for him again...
He's right.

This could be our second chance at love...
Or maybe I'm about to get burned all over again.

This full-length romance is packed with heart and heat! A brooding hero and the woman he loves. His four fun-loving brothers, small town characters, and a swoony ending will leave you more than satisfied. :)

Click here and get Come Back to Me now!

COME BACK TO ME SNEAK PEEK

Description

Ten years ago he broke my heart and my cherry.
Never saw him again.
Until I showed up to work today.

Gavin Cole was my first everything.
Smoldering hot with a drop-your-panties grin.
Our future was bright…
Until he shattered my world.
I left town and closed the door on love.

Now I'm back in our small town.
Mr. Hotter-Than-Ever is my new boss.
And he's determined to make me his.

I built mile-high walls around my heart.
If he thinks he can parade his chiseled abs around
and make me fall for him again...

He's right.
And that might just be my ruin.

This could be our second chance at love...
Or maybe I'm about to get burned all over again.

Click here to get Come Back to Me now!

PROLOGUE

JOLIE

Ten Years Ago

The worst day of my life started out on such a high note.

I couldn't stop grinning as I waited for my boyfriend to pick me up for school. I was on top of the world, and with good reason.

A new world was right around the corner. High school graduation, freedom, and moving to the city.

Best of all, I'd be with the love of my life.

Little did I know, he was about to break my heart.

"Looking good, babe!" Gavin shouted through the open window of his truck.

He pulled his old Ford Bronco to the curb in front of my house, just as he did every morning. His blue eyes locked on mine, and my heart did a flip.

I waved goodbye to my mom, who watched from the doorway.

"Hi, Mrs. Adams!" Gavin called to her.

"You kids behave yourselves," she said, smiling, before she closed the front door.

"What are you all dressed up for?" he asked as I hopped in the passenger side.

Our friends Anna and Ryan were in the backseats. As always, the seat next to Gavin was reserved for me.

I shrugged. "It's our last week of high school. I guess I'm just excited."

I was wearing the dress he'd given me for my eighteenth birthday. It was a peach floral print that reached to my midcalf. It was just my style, even if it was fancier than what I usually wore to school.

I leaned toward Gavin and gave him a quick kiss. "Good morning!" I said brightly.

Gavin smiled. "Good morning yourself, gorgeous. Got another of those for me?"

"For you, baby? I happen to have an unlimited supply," I said.

Ryan made a gagging sound from the backseat. I ignored it. Leaning toward Gavin, I kissed him longer this time.

"Um, sorry to interrupt your tongue wrestling match," Anna said, "but could you two maybe be just a little less nauseating? I mean, my mom makes a great breakfast, but I'm not sure I feel like tasting it twice in one morning."

"Oh, you're just jealous because your boyfriend isn't as handsome as mine," I teased.

Anna turned to Ryan, elbowing him in the ribs. "Hey! Aren't you supposed to be offended by that remark?"

Ryan shrugged. "What can I say? I'm not so insecure in my masculinity that I won't admit it: Gavin's a damn good-looking guy. If I weren't straight, I'd date him."

"Gee, thanks for that, man," Gavin replied, glancing at him in the rearview mirror with an amused grimace. "If I get any unsigned cards on Valentine's Day next year, I guess I'll know where they came from, huh?"

"So, what's the news from around town today?" I asked. It was a game we often played on the way to school.

"Wow, I mean, where to start?" Gavin smirked. "The mailman was pretty sure he saw a woodchuck behind his house. They called a town meeting about that one."

"And Kurt from the hardware store bought a new weed whacker," Anna chimed in with a grin. "CNN sent a camera crew to cover that."

"Don't forget about the new coat of paint that's drying on the door of the post office," Ryan said, laughing. "Thrilling stuff. I'll definitely be watching that later, if I can handle that kind of excitement."

"God, it's going to feel so good to get out of this town and live in a real place for once!" I exclaimed happily. "After this summer, it'll be Roanoke and parties and music! No more counting off the days in a place where nothing ever happens except tourist season."

"Tourist season, ha," Ryan scoffed. "Won't be missing that either. Bunch of obnoxious out-of-towners getting drunk all summer, puking in the streets, and nearly drowning in the lake. Remember that guy who fell off the charter boat last summer? Geez."

"Those people might suck, granted," Gavin reminded him, "but without them, my dad wouldn't have made nearly as much money from all his hotels."

"Yeah, that really seemed to make him happy, too," Anna said sarcastically.

A shadow passed over Gavin's face, and we all fell into an awkward silence. His father Robert's ruthless and miserly nature had been a long-running joke in our little town of North Haven, Virginia. We had made comments like Anna's ever since we were all kids, even Gavin himself.

His dad had been the richest man in town. He'd also been the most unpopular, considered by many to be callous and greedy. He wasn't the best father to Gavin and his brothers, either.

But Gavin's parents had been killed by a drunk driver only a year before. Sometimes, it was a bit too easy for us to forget that he was still dealing with the grief.

"Hey, I'm sorry," Anna said, reaching forward and squeezing Gavin's shoulder. "That was a shitty thing for me to say."

He gave her a small smile that didn't reach his eyes. "It's okay. Really. And you're right. The fact that he's dead now doesn't mean he wasn't kind of a prick while he was alive."

I put a hand on his knee to comfort him, and he looked over at me gratefully.

"Everything's going to be okay," I told him. "Soon, we'll be off to college together, and we'll be able to put this whole place behind us and start our actual lives."

"Damn right," he said, giving me a smile. "Can't wait."

God, he was so handsome and loving and amazing. Sometimes I had a hard time believing that he was my boyfriend. How could I have been so lucky to find someone like Gavin? He'd never done anything to shake my faith in our relationship over the course of three years.

I'd found the perfect guy.

The previous month, when I had given him my virginity, he had been so gentle, so tender, so concerned with making sure I was really ready. It had been a little fumbling and awkward like most first times probably were, but it had still been amazing because it was with him.

And we had so much more of that ahead of us!

I leaned close, whispering in his ear playfully, "Soon, we won't have to sneak around after my mom goes to sleep. We can just go to each other's dorm rooms to have sex, like normal people."

He grinned from ear to ear. "I'll have to come up with

some way to let my roommate know when you're there so he doesn't walk in on us."

"There's the old hang a sock on the doorknob trick," Anna suggested helpfully.

"Yeah," Ryan snickered, "or the old hang up a sign that says We're Boning In Here, Come Back In Two Minutes trick."

"You're such an asshole." Gavin laughed.

I loved his smile. I couldn't wait to spend the rest of my life doing everything I could to make sure he did it as often as possible.

First Roanoke University, I thought happily, and then the world!

He pulled into the parking lot of North Haven High, and I jumped out of the truck. "I've got to run on ahead. I did this extra credit assignment for Ms. Maxwell, and I have to get it in to her before the bell."

"Cool, I'll catch up with you later!" Gavin called after me.

"See you soon," I said as I hurried off.

I glanced back to see him bending down to inspect some minor scratch on the body of the Bronco.

Gavin's father had hated that twenty-year-old vehicle when he'd been alive. He could never understand why his son hadn't wanted something new and sleek. But Gavin loved that old truck. He'd fixed it up and made it just as nice as anything new.

"It's a classic," he'd tell anyone who would listen.

I smiled to myself. I could hardly wait for our life together to begin.

As I bounded up the front steps of the school, I started to feel weird, like everyone spoke in a whisper as soon as I'd gotten close.

I looked around.

Everyone was staring at me. Some of them appeared to be

horrified, a few of them were trying to stifle laughter, but all of their eyes were on me. They all knew something I didn't.

Dread filled my chest. I didn't know what was waiting for me on the other side of that door, but something inside me was too afraid to take another step. It wanted me to turn and run away as fast as I could, to make up any excuse—that I was suddenly sick or that I had a family emergency. Anything to get away from that awful sea of eyes blinking at me.

Instead, I summoned all my courage, put my hand on the metal bar of the door, and pulled it open.

The walls and lockers were all heavily papered with copies of the same black and white photograph. Several faculty members were yanking them down by the fistful as quickly as possible, while the students just stared at them.

And at me.

"Jolie!" Ms. Maxwell hurried down the hall toward me, dropping an armload of the photos into a nearby trash can. She had a worried expression on her face. "Jolie, no, don't come in yet! Wait outside, please! Everything's all right, but just wait."

I looked at the photo on those pages. The picture was so surreal to me, so unbelievable, that it took my mind a few seconds to process it.

When I finally did—when I understood what I was looking at—I felt my entire world shatter, like a crystal ornament dropped on the floor.

Then, I did turn and run. As fast as my legs could carry me.

In some ways, I wasn't sure I ever stopped.

Grab your copy of COME BACK TO ME now!

CHAPTER 1

GAVIN

*M*adison's skirt was short.

Again.

It was even shorter than it had been the previous day, which I hadn't realized was possible since that one was so high that it had seemed like little more than a thick belt around her waist.

This one was practically a ribbon.

She wanted me to notice, and of course I did. But from the way she bent over the desk to put paperwork in front of me—the sensual smiles she gave me and the astonishingly obvious come-hither look in her eyes whenever they met mine—I knew that she also wanted a lot more than that.

And what she wanted would make things complicated. Which I didn't need.

So I did my best to keep my eyes on my desk. I didn't want to encourage her. I figured if I stuck to my guns long enough, she'd get bored and find someone else to wiggle those hips at.

Kevin Banks sat across from me. His eyes were shamelessly locked on her curves. He waited for her to be out of earshot then let out a low whistle. "Oh man, please tell me you're getting a slice of that on a regular basis."

"Nope." I made a show of studying the blueprints for what would be my newest—and most luxurious—hotel.

"You're kidding!" he balked. "Why the hell not? Didn't you see the way she was looking at you? She clearly wants you!"

I sighed, putting the blueprints aside. "Yes. But Madison wants the whole silly scenario. She wants me to ask her to work late, suggest we order in dinner, share some jokes. And somewhere along the way, it all turns into rolling around on the floor among the manila folders and contracts."

"So?" Kevin chuckled. "What's the problem with that?"

"The problem is, I've fallen for it before. And I'm sick of having to hire a new assistant every few months. Because after the sex, they want relationships."

"Well, if you don't want her, I'll take her."

"You have my blessing to give it a shot," I said, looking at the blueprints again. "But—no offense—I don't think you're Madison's type."

Kevin's eyes wandered down to his beer belly and a hand fluttered over his balding scalp. He cleared his throat.

"Now, if you don't mind," I said. "I'd like to get back to finalizing the location of the new hotel."

Kevin raised an eyebrow. "What's to finalize? The location is obvious. You want it on Lake Moore, and the perfect lot for the hotel is available on the west side of it. A bit pricey, sure, but not beyond your means, especially given how much you'll make when it opens. That spot will give your guests the best view of the lake and put them close enough to the water for you to set them up with water taxi tours, charter fishing, the whole shebang."

"I want the hotel on the east side of the lake," I said flatly.

"It doesn't make sense, though. The west side has the better view," Kevin protested.

He was right about the lake views of the western lot. But it wasn't just the lake that brought tourists. North Haven was set in a picturesque valley of the Blue Ridge Mountains of southern Virginia. The views were stunning every way a person looked. Not to mention the charm that the town had to offer. It was why my business tycoon father had picked North Haven to develop before I was born.

"You told me all that already," I reminded him. "And I told you, find another spot."

Kevin blinked at me, confused. "Okay, well, maybe if I knew why you object to building on that lot, I'd be in a better position to provide you with alternatives."

I knew full well that Kevin didn't give a shit about providing me with alternatives. He was just damn nosy, like the rest of the busybodies in North Haven. In a town that size, none of the locals ever minded their own business. During the off season, when the tourists weren't around to raise hell, gossip was the only real source of entertainment for most of the people who lived there year-round.

Still, I supposed I had to tell him, if that was what it took for him to drop the subject and look for a different location.

"Teresa Adams lives next to that lot," I said. "It would make her unhappy."

"Yeah, no shit," Kevin snorted. "But your hotel will make all the locals unhappy. They already think your resorts are taking up too much lakefront space. Why should she be any different?"

He had a point. I usually didn't care about who I disturbed by putting my buildings where I did. My father hadn't become a business mogul by worrying about every little guy he came across. Cole Enterprises was still thriving, even after he was gone. And that was because I was willing to do just about anything to keep it going.

But this property was different.

I stood up and turned to look out the window.

When this had been Dad's office, it had been all expensive woods—mahogany desk and stately chairs. Even wooden pens, which had been bizarre to me.

When he'd actually spent time with me during his life, Dad had always told me I needed to be more styled and put together with everything from my first beat-up truck to my clothes. I'd gotten rid of the truck in college, and I'd cleaned up my look well before business school.

And a few years ago, when I'd taken over the business from the trustees that had managed it after my parents' death, I'd had the office redone in sleek lines. All grays, blacks, and leathers. But its modern, pristine look made it uncomfortable. I often found myself restless.

"Kevin, you're the best commercial building contractor in three counties. You've built my last two hotels for me. I want you to build this one, and hopefully a whole bunch more down the line. But in order for that to happen, I suggest you propose a different location."

"Or what?" he laughed. "You'll hire Donald Markinson and his crew of drunks? Or hey, I'm sure you could get a good estimate from Phil Baxter. This past year, I heard that he actually had four of his projects up to code out of ten."

I spun around and eyed him.

He raised his hands defensively. "Come on, Gavin, there's no need to play hardball. I'm just trying to help! I need to know what you're thinking so I can do that. I mean, what if there's something about the next lot I ask you to consider that would somehow piss her off too?"

I rolled my eyes. "Fine. If you must know, it would seriously lower the value of Teresa Adams's house. She's getting older, and she might decide to sell it someday if she needs the money. And if she does, she should be able to get as much as possible for it. Besides, putting a six-story hotel there would block her view of the lake. That view always meant a lot to her."

Kevin tilted his head. "Wow. Okay. How do you know so much about Mrs. Adams?" Before I could answer, he snapped his fingers, remembering. "Oh, that's right! Didn't I once hear that you used to date her daughter in high school? What was her name again? Janie? Julie?"

"Jolie."

Just uttering the name out loud made me feel like I had a bone stuck in my throat. All the old memories were coming back, whistling through the air, and burying themselves deep in my heart like daggers.

"So, hang on. Is that what this thing with the Adams lady is about?" Kevin demanded. "Are you still sweet on this Jolie chick after all these years? Yikes, man. I guess that would also explain why you aren't hopping all over Madison like a bunny in springtime, huh? I mean, ten years, that's a hell of a long time to still be carrying a torch."

I gritted my teeth. What could I say to him? That I had never lived down the guilt of how I had hurt her? That no matter how many years went by, all it took was the sudden memory of her humiliation—the look that twisted her face to tears as she ran out of the school and pushed past me—to make me brood for days? Ten years, and the pain was still as sharp as it had been on the day it happened.

If I had known that those kisses in the car would be the last ones we'd ever have, I wouldn't have gone to classes that day. I'd have dropped off Anna and Ryan and spent the whole rest of the day with her. I'd have tried to somehow make those hours last forever.

But since Jolie had left town after graduation—angrily vowing never to speak to me again—I figured trying to look out for her mother's best interests was the very least I could do.

If that meant making sure her property value didn't get destroyed, so be it.

She'd been like a second mother to me when my world fell apart after my parents' deaths. She deserved any help I could give her.

Madison poked her head in, her blonde hair framing the look of concern on her face. "Sorry, I don't mean to interrupt, but did I hear you guys talking about Teresa Adams?"

"No need to apologize, darling. You can interrupt me anytime!" Kevin said with a lascivious wink. I was half surprised he didn't pat his lap and offer her a seat there. "And yes, as a matter of fact, we were discussing Mrs. Adams. What about her?"

"Well, I see her at the grocery store sometimes, and whenever we've chatted, she's been really nice," Madison said, her mouth a fretful little red O as she sat on the couch. "And I just think it's really sad, you know? What she's been going through."

"What? Dealing with the prospect of seeing a luxury hotel whenever she looks out the window?" Kevin grunted derisively. "Hardly a tragedy, wouldn't you say? More of a mild inconvenience, when you come right down to it."

"Oh no." Her eyes widened. "You didn't hear what happened?"

"I know that her husband left her," I answered, trying to keep my tone neutral.

Kevin chortled. "Wow, you really have been keeping tabs on this lady, haven't you, buddy?"

"But that was almost a year ago," I went on, ignoring his comment. "Surely she's recovered from that since then."

"No, not that," Madison replied, wincing. "She got diagnosed with breast cancer. And I heard it was pretty bad."

I sat back in my chair, feeling all the air leave my lungs at once. "No, Madison. I hadn't heard that."

I cleared my throat and then stood up and crossed to the door.

"We're done here, Kevin. Find me a different lot."

I opened the door and waited as Kevin blinked then nodded.

"Whatever you say, Gavin," he said. He scampered to his feet and walked out the door.

Madison lounged on the couch and gave me a sly smile.

"Bye, Madison," I said as I jerked my head toward the door. She dropped the seductive look abruptly before hurrying out the office.

I returned to the window and sighed.

I wondered when Jolie had heard this news and how she had taken it. She must have been devastated. I wanted to look up her phone number, to call her, to make sure she was all right.

Except I knew that hearing from me would probably just make her feel worse.

No, the best thing I could do for her at that point was make sure she never had to see me—or even think about me—ever again.

No matter how difficult that prospect was for me.

As hard as I'd tried to forget her over the past ten years, Jolie's memory was seared in my mind.

The first, and only, girl I'd ever loved.

Grab your copy of COME BACK TO ME now!

Made in the USA
Las Vegas, NV
12 August 2021